THOSE
PEOPLE
NEXT
DOOR

Also by Kia Abdullah

Next of Kin
Truth Be Told
Take It Back

THOSE PEOPLE NEXT DOOR

Kia Abdullah

ONE PLACE. MANY STORIES

For my big sis, Shopna, without
whom I would not be a writer

PART I

Chapter One

Salma had never thought that she would end up living in a street like this. It looked too shiny and new, like a row of plastic dolls' houses. When she and her husband had first come to view it, they had joked about the name of the street. 'Hampton' made it sound like a palace when really it was charmless, and barely inside London.

Six months and forty houses later, they realised that nothing else matched Hampton for price, space and safety. *Four double bedrooms*, said her husband, Bil. *And it's still on the Central line. The neat streets and quiet neighbours*. Maybe they could be happy here. They had talked each other into it – and now here they were, at their first barbecue with neighbours.

Salma, Bil and their son, Zain, hovered at the edge of the garden. There were about thirty guests there. Two men were looking after the barbecue and cheers went up around them as they served the first round of meat, filling the air with a pleasant smoky smell.

A woman hurried over to Salma. 'You must

be the new arrivals!' She pulled her into a hug. 'I'm Linda Turner, the hostess.' The woman was in her late fifties and wore a roomy floral dress over her plump frame.

'Hello! I'm Salma. Thank you so much for inviting us.'

'I'm Bilal,' said her husband. He saw Linda's frown and quickly added, 'Call me Bil.'

'Bil! How wonderful. And this must be your son. My, what a handsome boy!'

Zain smiled politely. 'How do you do?'

Linda whooped with delight. 'And such manners too!'

Zain offered her the bowl in his hands. 'We brought some potato salad.'

'You didn't have to bring anything!' She took the bowl. 'What can I get you to drink? We have wine, beer, cider.' She paused. 'Or we have fresh lemonade and fruit juice.'

Bil smiled. 'A lemonade would be lovely. Thank you.'

'Make that three,' said Salma.

'Wonderful!' Linda called over a nearby guest. 'This is Tom Hutton. He lives next door to you. He will look after you.'

Tom greeted them warmly. He was in his mid-forties, muscular, and had thick dark hair underneath an orange cap. As he spoke, a bull terrier came up to him. 'Her name is Lola,' he said, bending down to pet her. 'She was a showgirl.'

Salma recognised the lyrics from Barry Manilow's hit song and laughed. Tom nodded with approval as if she had passed a test. Lola fussed around Salma's feet.

'You don't mind, do you?' said Tom.

'No, not at all. We have a dog too. A labrador called Molly.'

'Oh, that's great. This is such a dog-friendly neighbourhood. You're going to love it.'

Linda returned with drinks and whisked Bil away to help with the barbecue. Zain drifted to a corner with his phone.

'So what do you do?' asked Tom.

'I teach geography at a secondary school,' said Salma. 'What about you?'

'I work in advertising. At Sartre & Sartre.'

'Oh wow. That must be glamorous.'

'It can be.' Tom grinned, enjoying the compliment. 'What about your husband?'

Salma tensed. 'Bil is a restaurateur,' she said, despite the fact that his restaurant, Jakoni's, had shut down earlier that year.

'Wow. You must be doing all right then, no?'

Salma gave a little laugh. 'We're doing okay.'

'How come you got this place then?' He gestured in the direction of their house.

Salma relaxed. She was pleased to find that Tom was unsure about Hampton too. She smiled playfully. 'It's not so bad, is it? Where else would I find such a perfect collection of lawns?'

Tom frowned. 'It's just that I would have thought you were above the threshold.'

'Threshold?'

'For social housing,' he said.

It dawned on Salma what Tom had meant: not *you're rich so why would you choose to live here* but *you're rich so why did you get social housing*? 'Um, we actually bought it privately,' she told him.

'Oh!' Tom clearly felt bad. 'God, I'm sorry. I didn't mean to assume. I could have sworn that the house next to us was part of the social housing.'

Salma waved away the mistake. 'Oh, if only! It would have saved us a lot of money.' She laughed but it sounded hollow. She was thankful when Tom's wife joined them. She was tall with white-blonde hair, sharp cheekbones and a tiny gap between her front teeth.

'I'm Willa,' she said. 'Like the writer.'

Salma shook her hand and pretended to know which writer she meant.

'Although I work more with pictures.'

'Oh. Are you a model?'

Willa laughed. 'You're sweet, but no. I paint sometimes. Mainly, I run our home.'

'You look like you could be,' said Salma. 'You must get that all the time.'

Willa rolled her eyes. 'Thank you, but it's fucking embarrassing. I'm like a Nazi's fantasy.'

Salma nearly spat out her lemonade. She looked at Tom but he didn't react. Instead, he slid his arm around Willa's waist. Salma cleared her throat. 'Do you have kids?' she asked, changing the subject.

'Yes. Jamie. He's sixteen.'

'My son, Zain, is eighteen,' said Salma. 'I'm sure he would love to meet Jamie.'

'That would be lovely,' said Willa.

They made small talk until a natural lull allowed Salma to excuse herself. She scanned the crowd and found Bil with Linda, the hostess.

'What is that delicious nutty flavour in the potato salad?' Linda was asking.

'Fried pine nuts,' Salma answered.

'Ah, well, thank you for indulging us. Just so you know, I can handle my spice so if you ever want to bring something with a bit more zing, you would be more than welcome to.'

Salma caught Bil's eye. 'Of course.'

Linda clapped her hands like an excited child. 'I look forward to it.' She glanced over Salma's shoulder. 'Well, I should mingle. Please have more food. There's so much to get through.'

Salma and Bil stayed for another hour, but left as soon as it was polite to. Zain walked on ahead and left the front door open for them. Salma paused by their lawn, which Tom had mowed while the house was for sale. She kicked a few pebbles back onto the path and picked up a palm-sized banner from the ground that Zain had stuck in a plant pot. She dug it back in place and followed Bil inside. She closed the door and sagged against it.

Bil laughed. 'Are you okay?'

'Yes, but that was *a lot* to face in one go.'

Bil winced with sympathy. 'You don't regret moving here, do you?'

There was a tiny pause before she spoke. 'No. I think we can be happy here.' Salma had tried to stay positive ever since Jakoni's shut down in January after an awful year for the restaurant business. In truth, she *did* worry that they had made a mistake. If they had known that they would lose the restaurant, they might have stayed in Seven Kings among other Bangladeshi families. By the time Jakoni's closed, however, they were tied into buying the house in Hampton. They hadn't yet managed to sell the restaurant and money was getting tight.

Salma reminded herself that they didn't have a choice. Not after what happened with Zain. He had space to breathe here: a large bedroom, his own bathroom, a balcony and a garden too. They would fit in before long. They had to. They had nowhere else to go.

Chapter Two

Zain took a drag of his cigarette and blew smoke into the night air. His thoughts went to the barbecue and the question that people kept asking: what do you do?

I'm a student, he had told them, hating himself for lying. The truth was that he had been kicked out of college last year, which meant that he couldn't sit his A levels or go to university. He lived with his parents like a deadbeat and spent Friday nights on Twitch, live-streaming his computer coding.

He took another drag of his cigarette, then heard a cough next door. A boy leaned out past the brick column between their balconies. He was close to Zain's age, white, and looked like he belonged in a boy band.

Zain stubbed out his cigarette. 'Shit. Sorry, mate.'

'It okay.' The boy stretched across the column. 'I'm Jamie.'

'Zain.' They shook hands.

'So, what brought you to paradise?'

'The search for a better life,' joked Zain.

'Ha! Prepare to be disappointed.'

Zain smiled. 'How long have you lived here?'

'We moved here when I was nine, so seven years now. It not bad.'

Zain noticed that Jamie dropped the 's' from 'it's'. *It not bad. It okay.* He wondered if the boy had a speech problem.

'But I can't wait to leave,' said Jamie.

'And go where? Uni?'

'Start my own company maybe.'

Zain laughed, but then saw the look of hurt on Jamie's face. 'Sorry, I just— It's not that easy, is it?'

Jamie frowned. 'No, you're right. It's stupid.'

'Nah, man. It's not stupid. It's better than working for someone else,' Zain backtracked and felt guilty. 'Do you have an idea?'

'Kind of.' Jamie fidgeted. 'I could show you?' He went into his room and came back a few seconds later. Shyly, he handed Zain a stack of designs. 'It's an app that translates sign language into speech to help deaf people talk to hearing people.'

Zain raised his brows to show the younger boy that he was impressed. 'How come you're interested in this?'

'Well, you might not be able to tell, but I'm partially deaf. I was born premature, but they didn't realise anything was different until I was four. By then, certain sounds were lost to me. I wanna do something to help others like me.'

'Good on you, man.' Zain looked through the designs. 'Grapevine?' he said, spotting the name. 'As in "I Heard It Through the Grapevine"? Clever.'

Jamie blushed. 'Thanks. I just need to find someone to build it now.'

Zain looked up. 'You know I can do computer code, right?'

'Really? Would you be interested?'

Zain considered this. 'I mean, *maybe*.' He studied the designs again and asked a few more questions. 'Okay,' he said finally. 'Why the hell not?'

'Man, that would be fantastic.' Jamie reached out his hand again.

Zain shook it and something warm pitched inside him: a sense of purpose and comradeship.

There was a call from inside Jamie's house. 'Shit, that's Mum. I better go. Here, take my number.'

Zain put it in his phone and listened to Jamie go. He looked out over the inky grass and felt a new sense of hope.

Chapter Three

Salma hurriedly tied her hair in a bun. The strands at the back came loose, but she didn't have time to fix it. She checked that she had her keys and wallet and gave Bil a kiss goodbye.

'Don't you want breakfast?' he asked.

'Sorry. I've got to get in early,' said Salma, feeling guilty. When Jakoni's shut down, Bil took an entry-level job at a local curry house. He worked exhausting split shifts, but still woke up every morning to make her breakfast. 'I'll grab an apple instead,' she told him.

Downstairs, she found Zain on his laptop at the kitchen table.

'Hey Zain, tape this up for me, would you?' She tapped a cardboard box. 'Just be careful. They're your dad's knives from Jakoni's. He's selling them to Suli.' A look passed between them. Bil giving up his cherished knives felt like a sign of surrender – but they needed the money.

She listed some other chores for Zain and gave him a kiss goodbye. Outside, she noticed that his banner was on the ground again. *Black Lives*

Matter, it said, printed black on pink. She had been unsure when Zain first displayed it. She and her family were Asian – not Black – and she didn't want to cause a fuss.

'I think we should meet the neighbours first before we put up something like that,' she had said.

'Because *that* will inform whether Black lives matter?' Zain had replied with scorn.

'Just put it somewhere not too in-your-face,' she had told him.

Now, she picked it up and stuck it back in the plant pot. As she headed to the bus stop, she heard a beep to her left. Her neighbour, Tom, was in his car and she raised a hand to wave. He rolled down his window and beckoned her closer.

'Morning, Salma.'

'Hi, Tom. How are you?'

'Good, good.' He took off his sunglasses. 'Listen, can I ask a favour?' He grimaced as if this pained him. 'Can you guys try to park in front of *your* house?'

Salma looked at her car, which overshot her house by a foot. 'Oh, sorry! I didn't realise there was designated parking.'

'No, no. There isn't. It's just that we have two cars so if you overshoot, we can't get both of ours in.'

'Oh.' Salma frowned. 'Well, sometimes people park outside ours, so we roll forward a bit so our car will fit.'

'Ah. Maybe you could find out who's doing it and have a word?'

'Um, sometimes it's different cars.'

'Okay, well …' He tapped the steering wheel as if trying to find an answer. 'If you can't figure out who it is, then that's fine, but it *is* a bit of a pain for us to park around the corner.'

'Okay, sure. We'll try our best.' Salma moved to go, but Tom stopped her.

'Sorry. While I'm being annoying, I should say that the fence between our gardens has a loose board. We fixed it last time, and then again when the house was empty, so maybe you guys could have a look at it?'

'Of course.'

'Great.' He beamed. 'Thanks for understanding. Have a good morning.'

'You too,' she said, her cheeks burning. Surely it wasn't fair to claim a part of the road just because it passed your home? She wished that she hadn't agreed so easily. Or at least made a pointed joke to show him this wasn't okay. Next time, she would speak her mind.

Chapter Four

Zain waited as Jamie stepped around the central column that stuck out between their balconies. He reached up to help but Jamie jumped down easily. Zain led him inside and felt a little embarrassed by the neatness of his room. His computer books were stacked on his desk in a straight line. His shoes were in a tidy row and even the smell – a faint lemongrass from the oil his mum liked – seemed girly. It didn't quite fit the image of a computer genius. They sat side by side at the desk and began to work on an application for money for Grapevine from Google's diversity fund. When it came to the section about disability, Zain looked across at Jamie.

'Hey man, is it hard? Being deaf?'

Jamie shrugged. 'It can be, but you have to get over it. I used to try to hide it, but my tutor said it's easier if you're upfront. Sometimes it's not nice when waiters and people get impatient with me, but if I point out my hearing aids, usually they're nicer.'

Zain leaned forward. 'You can barely see them.'

Jamie fiddled with one. 'They're new. In primary school, I used to have these massive ones. It was so embarrassing.'

'And now?'

'Sometimes I'm embarrassed, but not as much. I'm okay in shops and cinemas and ordering stuff, but I still don't really …' he hesitated '… talk to girls and stuff.'

Zain laughed. 'Is there a specific one we're talking about?'

Jamie blushed. 'Her name's Camilla. I knew her in primary and she was always nice to me, but in secondary she's been a bit off.'

'In what way?'

'Like if I don't hear something in class, she used to be nice but now she laughs with everyone else. Sometimes, I have to guess at the bit I missed. When I get it wrong, they laugh. Like if the teacher asks, "Is this A or B?" and I say "Yes" because I haven't understood.'

Zain felt a pang of sorrow. He wanted to reach out and touch him somehow – an arm around his shoulders, a squeeze of support – but their friendship did not yet have that ease. Instead, he punched him softly on the arm. 'Well, let's see how Camilla likes you when Grapevine earns us millions.'

Jamie pretended to pop his collar, and the

awkward way that he did it filled Zain with affection.

'Speaking of girls, teach me how to sign some chat-up lines.'

Jamie laughed. 'What are you going to do? Hit up a girl at deafPLUS?' Jamie tutored a group at the centre each Friday.

'Why not? I'm an equal opportunity Casanova.' Zain ducked and weaved like a boxer.

'Please don't do that in front of her.'

Zain elbowed him. 'Come on. I can help you find a girlfriend.'

'I have Lola for that. All the girls there love her.'

Zain shook his head. 'Upstaged by a fucking dog.'

They both laughed, warm in the glow of a friendship that hadn't yet been tested.

Chapter Five

Salma clumsily climbed into the Uber with her grocery bags. She hated to waste money on a taxi, but had bought too much to carry. It was a short drive along Horns Road and they arrived at Hampton within ten minutes, parking across from Salma's house. She climbed out and dragged the bags towards her. A tin of beans spilled out and rolled under the car.

'Sorry!' she called to the driver. 'Can you give me a minute?'

'Of course, miss.' He cut the engine. 'Take your time.'

Salma bent and reached for the tin. Across the street, a flicker caught her eye. Tom Hutton was in his front garden, throwing a yellow tennis ball from one hand to the other. Casually, he walked to the fence that divided his garden from Salma's. He glanced up and down the street, looking right past the Uber. He lifted the ball and threw it into her garden. It knocked Zain's banner out of the plant pot and rolled across the lawn.

The whole thing was so quick that Salma nearly

missed it. She blinked, not quite able to understand what she had just seen. Tom looked up and down the street again, then went into his house.

'You all right, miss?' called the driver.

'Yes, sorry!' Salma grabbed the tin. 'Thank you!' She stepped back and the car moved off. There, alone in the open street, she felt uncomfortably exposed. She hurried across the road, picked up the tennis ball and brought it inside along with the crumpled banner. Bil was in the hallway, unclipping Molly's leash.

'Hi, honey. Good day?' he asked.

'Something weird just happened.' Salma put down the banner and explained what she had seen.

Bil frowned. 'You saw him pull out the banner?'

'He threw the ball and knocked it out.'

Bil relaxed. 'Well, hon, clearly it was an accident.'

'It wasn't. Tom looked up and down the street to make sure no one was watching, then literally took aim. I've found the banner on the ground twice before, so it must have been him.'

'Maybe it was just a lark. You know how men are.'

'A lark?' asked Salma.

'Men see things and they want to take aim at them. Look at urinals. They paint a dot on them to make us aim for it.'

Salma stared at him. 'Why are we talking about urinals?'

'I'm just saying, maybe it wasn't unfriendly.'

'In that case, he won't mind if I do this.' She picked up the banner and marched to the living room window. She stuck it to the glass facing outward.

Bil looked on with a grimace. 'Are you sure that's a good idea?'

'Yes,' snapped Salma. 'It's staying there.' She smoothed a crease in the banner and ignored her own nerves.

Chapter Six

Willa leaned against the doorframe and waited for Tom to come in from the garden. She wore high heels and her favourite little black dress. She wanted Tom to remember this in a few months' time, when she got big from the pregnancy.

He came out of the shed and paused when he saw her. 'What have I done to deserve this?' he asked with a grin.

She beckoned him inside. At the dinner table, she sipped from her glass coyly. 'I'm drinking lime and soda,' she said. 'Not wine.' She leaned on the table. 'Because I can't drink wine.'

Tom looked at her glass and it took him a moment to catch her meaning. 'No ...' he said in disbelief.

'Yes.'

'Are you serious?'

'Yes.'

'But are you *sure*?'

Willa nodded, her eyes shining.

Tom sprang off his chair and dropped to his knees beside her. He wrapped his arms around her and pressed his face to her stomach. 'How long have you known?'

'A week.'

He pulled away a little. 'A week?'

'Yes. I wanted to be sure first. We've had so many false alarms. '

'But …' He released her. 'You were drinking at the barbecue.'

'One or two is fine.'

'You've been smoking as well.'

'Only one.'

'Sweetheart, I've seen you smoke every day.'

Willa scowled. 'Not *every* day.'

Tom gripped her hand in his. 'Honey, I know it's not fair but we've got to keep our baby safe.'

'I *know* that,' she said sourly.

'Tell you what. I'll give up drinking too. For the whole nine months.'

Willa shuddered. 'Oh, God, don't do that. We don't *both* have to be bores.'

'Okay, but you promise?'

She sighed. 'Fine.'

He took her cigarettes from the mantelpiece. 'So these are gone?'

'Gone,' said Willa.

He aimed them at the bin and hit the target easily. 'Gone!' He poured her another lime and soda and opened a bottle of beer. 'Things will be so much better this time. We have a garden. A car. A spare bedroom.'

Willa felt a knot in her stomach. Jamie's early years weren't easy with the three of them in her crowded Camden flat, but the thought of raising a child here, in Hampton, felt somehow worse. 'Don't you miss those days though?'

He scoffed. 'What? Hitting my head on the ceiling every time I went downstairs? And your dad lording it over me that he was paying our rent? No, thank you.'

'But don't you miss being part of that life? Culture and art were right on our doorstep.'

'We're parents now. We have different concerns.'

Willa stared at the bin. When Tom wasn't looking, she would take back her cigarettes. She didn't plan to smoke them, but why should he tell her what to do?

Chapter Seven

Salma set the coffee to brew and opened the living room curtains. She neatened a fold in the fabric and then she froze. At first, she thought she was mistaken. Maybe it was a trick of the light. As she peeled the banner from the window, her skin grew hot with shock. The bottom-left pane was covered in white paint. She stood there for a minute, too stunned to move. Then she set down the banner and ran upstairs to get Bil.

He rubbed his fingers across the glass. 'Surely not.' He put on his slippers and went outside, Salma close behind. They stood side by side and stared at the paint.

'What should we do?' she asked.

He thought for a moment. 'There's some white spirit in the shed.'

'We shouldn't just clean it, Bil. We need to talk to Tom.'

'We can't accuse him without any proof.'

'So what do we do? Calmly live next door to a racist?'

Bil flinched. 'Shh,' he said urgently. 'Be careful, Salma. You can't just say that word.'

She made a face. 'My husband, the good immigrant.' She could tell he was insulted, but she didn't reassure him. Instead, she stepped over the low fence into Tom's front garden.

'Come on, Salma. We're new here and—'

'We don't want to "rock the boat". I get it, Bil, but this is *not* acceptable.' She rang Tom's doorbell, then knocked loudly.

After a minute, Tom answered it. He wore grey joggers and a loose white T-shirt, and his hair was rumpled with sleep.

'Hi.' He glanced at his watch. 'Is everything all right?'

'Can I have a word?' said Salma.

'Yes?' He didn't invite them in.

Salma pointed across the lawn. 'Our house has been vandalised.'

He followed Salma's finger, but then frowned. 'How so?'

'Bottom right window.'

He squinted. 'Oh. Right. I'm sorry to hear that. It's probably kids from down the estate.'

'It's not though, is it?' She saw a flicker of anger. Bil touched her arm, but she shrugged him off. 'I saw what you did with our banner.'

Tom looked confused. 'What banner?'

'I saw you, Tom. You knocked it into our garden.'

His face changed. He was getting cross. 'Have you read the neighbourhood guidelines? They say that banners aren't allowed outside.'

Salma was surprised. She had thought that she had the moral high ground. 'Okay, but why not tell me that like an adult? Why knock out my banner and leave it on the lawn?'

'Because I'm tired of people like you ruining our neighbourhood.'

Salma stared at him. 'People like me?'

Tom's eyes grew wide. 'I didn't mean it like *that*. I meant people who come here and don't read the rules.'

'It's okay, Tom. I know *exactly* what you meant.' Salma turned and marched back to her house.

While Bil went to get the white spirit, Salma took photos of the painted window from inside and outside the house. She opened the Twitter app on her phone, uploaded two pictures and wrote a caption.

Yesterday, I saw our neighbour knock out this banner and leave it on our lawn. I brought it inside and put it in our window. This morning, we woke up to this. Three cheers for tolerant Britain.

She added three icons of the England flag – the white and red of the St George's Cross – and then, she pressed 'post'.

Chapter Eight

Salma washed the last of the dishes and passed them to Zain for drying. In recent days, she had seen a spark return to her son. He was working on an app, he said, and Salma was grateful to see him busy. She and Bil had given him everything: private tutoring, after school clubs and mentoring, but when he was thrown out of college, he lost all motivation.

Now, it felt like he was finding his way again. She was proud of him and was about to tell him that when she heard their doorbell ring. It was followed by a violent thump. Salma switched off the tap and hurried to the hallway. Through the spyhole, she saw that it was Tom.

She grimaced and opened the door. 'How may I help you, Tom?'

'Who the hell do you think you are?' There was spittle on his lips.

Zain came into the hallway. 'Mum, what's going on?'

Tom shoved his phone at Salma and she saw her tweet on screen. '"Three cheers for tolerant

Britain"?' he said. 'You don't think I'm tolerant? You're having a laugh if you think that's true.'

Zain stepped out of the house, forcing Tom back. 'Stop shouting at my mum.'

'Step back, little man,' Tom snarled.

'Excuse me?'

'Go back and hide behind your mother.'

Salma cut in. 'Tom, you're an adult. Please don't threaten my son.'

Tom glared at her. 'I'm not "threatening" your son. Jesus Christ. You really do love playing the victim, don't you?'

Zain was now behind Tom. He started to film on his phone.

'And you call *me* intolerant?' Tom carried on. 'If I was intolerant, I'd tell your husband not to park in front of our house and I'd tell you to shut up that fucking dog of yours.' He pointed a finger in her face, his temper now smoking. 'I'd tell you to fix that fucking fence. And I'd tell you to keep your windows closed so you don't stink up our clothes with your cooking!'

The words landed like a gunshot. For a second, they stared at each other, both of them locked in shock. A breeze blew across the lawn, chilling Salma's skin. There was panic in Tom's face. At first, it seemed he would apologise but then his face hardened.

'I'm not being funny,' he said. 'I'm just telling you the truth. If you can't tell the truth any more, then this country really has gone to the dogs.'

'I think you should leave,' said Salma.

'It was just a fucking banner.'

'I said I think you should leave.'

'Oh, don't worry. I'm leaving but I'll tell you this: don't get involved with my family. Don't talk to us, look at us or fucking *post* about us online. Stay away from us or you'll see what I can do.'

Salma remained calm. 'I am perfectly happy to do that,' she said.

Tom sneered, then turned and stormed away.

Salma felt the tension leave her body. She was coated in sweat. She pulled Zain inside and closed the door, trying not to let him see her shake.

Chapter Nine

Tom took a seat at the conference table. He propped one knee on the other and pretended to fix a cufflink. It was what he thought of as his James Bond pose – cool and composed. He was about to call in the first job applicant when Isabella, his boss's assistant, looked into the room.

'Can I borrow you?' she said.

'I'm about to start an interview.'

'Mr Makinson wants to see you.'

Tom felt a crackle of unease. 'Do you know what it's about?' he asked. Their boss rarely summoned staff to his office.

Isabella ignored the question. 'Please follow me.' She led him to Makinson's office and left him to sweat outside. He knocked and waited nervously.

'Come in,' said a voice that Tom didn't recognise.

He walked in and was surprised to find that Makinson wasn't there. In his place was Vanessa, an executive at the agency. She also happened to be Makinson's daughter.

'Tom,' she said curtly.

'Vanessa,' he said with a nod. Then, 'Where's your dad?'

'Please take a seat.' She laced her fingers on the desk. 'Tom, are you friendly with your neighbours?' she asked.

Tom cleared his throat. 'Friendly enough,' he lied.

'So you've never told them that they "stink up" your clothes with their cooking?'

Tom blinked. 'Who told you that?'

Vanessa stood and looked out at the horizon. 'Do you know how my dad built this company? He's not the smartest, the strongest, the most inventive or nimble. What he *can* do is read the room. He can look at the current climate and adapt. Some call him a populist, but what's wrong with being popular?'

She turned. 'You're a fucking idiot, Tom. You should have read the room. Everyone out there is "woke" now, but you tell your Asian neighbour that she *stinks up your clothes* and you have the fucking stupidity to be caught on film?'

'Film?' Tom felt a rush of panic.

Vanessa pushed her laptop towards him. There, on-screen, was Tom looming above Salma. He was shouting at her: 'I'd tell you to shut up that fucking dog of yours. I'd tell you to fix that fucking fence. And I'd tell you to keep your windows

33

closed so you don't stink up our clothes with your cooking!'

Tom's panic swelled. He hadn't realised that Zain had been filming. 'It's not what it looks like,' he said feebly.

'How the fuck is it not what it looks like?' Vanessa spun the laptop back round. 'Do you know what they're saying? "Racism? In advertising? Sounds about white." "No doubt Sartre & Sartre are 'horrified' and will do much 'soul searching' before it's trebles all round at The Wolseley."' Vanessa watched him icily. 'Tom, you're fired.'

Tom's body jerked as if he'd been hit. 'Vanessa, I've worked for your dad for fifteen years. You can't just fire me.'

'You did this to yourself.'

'Vanessa, come on.' He wiped the sweat off his upper lip. 'Willa is pregnant. We've got a baby coming.'

'You should have thought about that before you behaved in that way.'

'Oh, come on, Vanessa. You've never left an Indian restaurant and worried about the smell on your coat?'

'I've not been filmed on camera yelling it at the waiter.'

Tom was hot with panic. He and Willa were already in so much debt. One month without his salary and they could easily sink. He would die before he went begging to her father. 'At least I had the balls to say it straight to that woman's face. As if you fucking weasels don't think twice about who you're renting your flats to. Didn't Daniel say *just the other day* that his tenants had turned the walls yellow?' He pointed a finger at her. 'You say you stand for freedom of speech, but you're being a fucking coward.'

'You need to learn when to stop, Tom.'

'Fuck you, Vanessa.'

'Oh, that's really mature. Well done for handling this like an adult.' She buzzed her intercom. 'David, Tom is ready to go.'

Tom was numb with disbelief. 'So that's it? After fifteen years, it's just—' He brushed his hands as if wiping off dirt. 'It's "fuck off" without even the dignity of Scott telling me personally?'

The security guard, David, opened the door and hovered next to Tom.

'Goodbye, Tom,' said Vanessa.

'So that's it? This is really how we're doing it?' Tom waited but Vanessa didn't answer. He burnt with rage as David led him out and escorted him to his desk. As he packed up his personal items, his thoughts turned to Salma. That bitch. *That fucking uppity bitch.*

Chapter Ten

It had been a long, hard day at work and Salma was glad to be almost home. She walked up Hampton and saw that Zain was out on the lawn. She called to him and when he looked up, he burst into tears.

'Mum, I can't find Molly.'

Panic surged inside her. 'When did you last see her?'

'I took her for a walk and then she came upstairs. I was due to stream on Twitch and she was getting under the rollers of my chair so I sent her downstairs. When I came down, I couldn't find her.'

Salma marched into the house. 'Molly?' she called. 'Molly!'

'Mum, don't you think I've tried that?' Zain's voice trembled when he spoke.

Salma searched the house. She tested the garden door and found it unlocked. 'Was this ajar?'

'I don't know. I think I opened it when I was looking for her.'

'Are you sure?'

'No, Mum, I'm not sure!'

'Do you think she was stolen?'

Zain gripped a tuft of his hair. 'She's an old mutt. She wouldn't be worth anything. I shouldn't have sent her downstairs.'

Salma went back out to the street. She pictured Molly bleeding in a ditch. Their sweet and skittish dog was out there alone. 'She must be somewhere.'

'But where? How could she just disappear?' Panic turned Zain's face sharp and mean.

'Everything okay?' a voice asked behind them. Linda, the hostess of the barbecue, stood on the kerb. Zain turned away from her, embarrassed by his tears.

'Our dog, Molly, is missing,' said Salma. 'Have you seen her anywhere?'

Linda tutted with sympathy. 'Oh dear. I'm afraid not, but I can ask the neighbourhood WhatsApp group.'

Salma grew still. She hadn't known that there was a neighbourhood group. 'That would be great, Linda. I'll send you a picture of Molly.' As she fiddled with her phone, Salma saw movement at Tom's window. A thought came to her. 'Could Molly have got into Tom's garden?'

'I can't see how that would happen,' said Linda.

Salma began to fret. 'There's a loose board in

the fence. We've been meaning to fix it. I didn't think Molly could fit through.' She looked at Linda. 'Do you think you could ask him?'

'He's in the WhatsApp group.'

'No, I mean knock on his door and ask him for me. Things are still tense between us.'

Linda looked annoyed. 'Well, that's just childish, Salma. Of course he's angry about the firing – he has a right to be – but he wouldn't take your dog.'

Salma blinked. 'The firing?'

'Haven't you heard?' Linda's voice was grave. 'Tom was sacked yesterday. Because of your video.'

Salma felt her stomach drop. If Tom had been angered by a simple banner, he would be *livid* now.

Chapter Eleven

Zain heard a knock and looked up to find Jamie on his balcony. He wore a thin T-shirt and was shivering in the wind. Zain opened the door and let him in. Neither of them spoke for a second.

'Dad lost his job yesterday,' Jamie said glumly.

Zain was tired from searching for Molly all evening and didn't have the energy for this.

'Dad shouldn't have said what he said, but you didn't have to put the video on the internet, Zain. You know what can happen these days.'

'I *had* to put it up,' said Zain. 'What else was I meant to do?'

'Think about me?'

Zain was surprised by Jamie's honesty. Back on the estate in Seven Kings, no boy would ever have said this. 'Look, I didn't want you involved in this but I *had* to do it, man.'

Jamie grimaced. 'Mum's so stressed out. The vibe at home is weird.'

'Then you can come and hang here.'

'My parents won't like it.'

Zain shrugged. 'Neither will mine but we don't have to tell them, do we?'

Before Jamie could answer, his phone pinged with a message – turned up loud because of his hearing. His face turned pale as he read it. 'Oh my God.' He looked up. 'We won the funding.'

'What?'

Jamie held out his phone. 'We won.'

Zain took it and read the email. 'We won? Oh my God, we fucking won!' He shot to his feet and the two of them hugged by instinct, quick but fierce. They had just won £30,000 from the Google diversity fund. The first half would hit Jamie's account tomorrow. They would get the second half once they uploaded a working demo in three weeks' time. 'Oh my God, I can *finally* buy a new laptop,' yelled Zain. An idea came to him. 'Hey, we could offer a reward for Molly! Like a thousand quid or something.'

The joy dimmed on Jamie's face. 'We can't do that, can we?'

'Why not? It's our money now. We can spend it where we need to.'

'Come on, man,' Jamie said with a little laugh. 'We can't do that.'

Zain stared at him. 'Can't or won't?'

'Can't.'

'Okay, maybe just five hundred then.'

'It's not the amount.' Jamie fiddled with his phone. 'We have to record how the money is spent.'

'Yeah, but they give us some leeway.'

'Not for spending on a dog!'

'She's not just a dog. She's …' Zain stopped, embarrassed by the sudden high pitch of his voice. 'It's just five hundred quid, man.'

'Maybe it could be a loan and you could pay it back?'

'A *loan?* That's my money too.'

'It's Grapevine's money.'

Zain realised that they hadn't made things official. All their agreements were verbal and Jamie had all the money. They had named him as the main founder because he was the deaf one. 'It's a bit weird that all of the money is in your account,' said Zain. 'Shouldn't we split it?'

Jamie felt awkward now. 'Look, I just want us to be careful with it. We can't spend it on dogs and shit.'

Dogs and shit? Zain felt his blood heat. 'Go fuck off, Jamie.'

Jamie stood there, not saying anything.

Zain shoved Jamie's shoulder, unable to deal with his anger. 'I said fuck off.' When Jamie still didn't speak, Zain snarled at him. 'What? Are you dumb as well as deaf?'

Jamie's face cracked with hurt. For a beat, neither of them moved or spoke. Then Jamie nodded and left without a word. Zain clung to his temper, knowing if he let it waver, it would cave right into shame.

Chapter Twelve

Salma parked on a side street and hurried to Jakoni's. Bil had sent her a text telling her to come to the restaurant straight after work. She found him outside, looking pale and clammy.

'Stu just left,' said Bil. Their cut-price estate agent was meant to be showing a buyer around today. 'Salma, he found squatters in the restaurant.'

Salma's breath caught in her throat. No one would buy a restaurant taken over by squatters. 'Should we call the police?'

Bil shook his head. 'The squatters have a right to be there. The police won't do anything.'

'Should we try to talk to the squatters?'

Bil's face was lined with worry. 'Maybe but I'll go up alone.'

'No way,' said Salma. 'I'm coming with you.'

'Okay, but stay back, would you? Stu seemed pretty rattled up there.'

Inside, they moved up the stairs quietly. Voices shouted over music. Gently, Bil turned the doorknob. The door flew open and a boy, or young man, faced them. He was gaunt with bony features, and was talking on his phone. Salma noticed that it was an old Nokia with two stickers on the back: a marijuana leaf above a glittery skull and crossbones. The boy hung up and glared at them.

'What do you want?'

Bil cleared his throat. 'You're in my property,' he said.

The boy grinned, revealing bad teeth. 'This is *my* property now.'

'Oi, Rich, what's going on?' Two of his friends joined him by the door.

Salma was about to speak when she heard a sound she knew well. 'Molly?' She moved forward, but Rich blocked her from entering. The dog barked again and this time Bil pushed forward. Rich tried to slam the door, but Bil threw his weight against it so that it flew back on its hinges. Molly came bounding up to them but Rich grabbed her by her bright blue collar. She barked in distress.

'That ain't no Molly. This here is Yoda.'

'Liar!' cried Salma. 'That's her collar.' She lunged for the boy but he pushed her back easily. He tugged Molly cruelly, making her whimper. Salma thought that she saw her limping. Bil charged forward, but the two boys wrestled him back. In the next instant, one pulled out a knife. There was something in the way he handled it that made them both stop still.

Bil's voice took on an eerie calm. 'Okay, fellas, things have got out of hand.'

'Get the fuck out,' said Rich.

Sweat dotted Bil's upper lip. 'Please just give us our dog and we'll get out of here.'

'That ain't happening.'

'Rich, come on, just give us Molly and we'll go.' Bil tried to sound casual.

Salma touched his shoulder. She knew that he wouldn't leave Molly, so she decided for him. She felt him tense beneath her palm and in that moment, she knew that he would go for the knife. 'No!' She pulled his shirt just as he began to charge. They both stumbled and Rich slammed the door shut. Bil rammed his shoulder against it, but Salma pulled him away. She dragged him down the stairs and out to their car as he trembled with fear and rage.

Chapter Thirteen

Salma cursed as she caught another red light. She had planned to beat the rush hour, but by the time she left school, it was well past five o'clock. All day, she had felt a low-level panic over Molly. She had phoned the police twice, but was told to wait for updates.

The traffic inched forward and a flash of orange caught Salma's eye. She looked up and saw Tom on the corner of Benton Road. He was with his son, Jamie, and they were both laughing. The picture was oddly comforting. Caught in a moment of tenderness, Tom didn't look so scary.

Jamie leaned towards Tom, who held out a lighter. Salma frowned. She didn't know that Jamie smoked. He tucked his phone into his back pocket so that he could cup the flame from the wind. Salma felt a jolt of fright when she saw the sticker on the phone: a golden skull and crossbones. She realised that the boy with Tom wasn't Jamie at all. He turned sideways and when he grinned, Salma saw his row of crooked teeth. The boy with Tom was Rich. Rich, the squatter who had taken over their restaurant. Rich who had taken Molly.

The traffic light turned green and a horn sounded behind Salma. Tom looked up and the two of them locked eyes. Salma's car lurched forward. She tried to find a place to stop but the flow of traffic carried her on. When she was finally able to do a U-turn, both Tom and Rich had gone.

Things began to click into place. Tom must have taken Molly and given her to Rich. Salma U-turned again, each mile further stoking her anger. She parked directly in front of Tom's house and stormed across his lawn.

'Tom!' She banged on his door. 'Can you open up please?'

A shadow emerged and Willa opened the door. Her face wrinkled as if she had caught a bad smell. 'May I help you?'

'Tom!' Salma yelled.

Willa drew back as if she had been slapped. 'Excuse me, can you not shout in my face please?'

Salma saw a flash of orange in the hallway.

Tom strode up and pulled Willa back to shield her. 'What the hell are you doing?'

'What the hell are *you* doing?' said Salma. 'You took our dog.'

He stared at her. 'What are you on about?'

'You took Molly and gave her to Rich. I saw you.'

'The lad with the bad teeth?' Tom smirked. 'You really have no clue, do you?'

'I saw you with him literally a minute ago!'

Tom sighed. 'If you must know, I was buying weed, okay?'

'You're lying,' said Salma. Just then, Tom's dog walked into the hall. Salma bent down and called her over. 'Lola, come here!'

Tom scowled. 'What are you doing?'

'Lola! Come on!' Salma's voice grew shrill.

Zain appeared on the lawn behind her. 'Mum? What's happening?'

Salma ignored them both. Instead, she grabbed Lola's collar. 'You've taken my dog so I'm taking yours.'

'Don't be so ridiculous.' Tom tried to take Lola but Salma swiftly escaped him. He reached again but she blocked him with her body. Tom grabbed her shoulders and pulled her backwards to get at Lola. His nails dug into flesh and Salma cried out in pain. Zain rushed forward and shoved Tom into Willa. She yelped as she fell and landed on an elbow. Then she began to shriek.

Tom was by her side in a flash. 'It's okay.' He tried to calm her. 'She'll be okay. I promise.'

She? Salma saw Willa cradle her belly. *Oh God. No.*

When the paramedics arrived, Willa told them that she was pregnant. Teary-eyed, she asked, 'When will the police get here?'

The paramedic looked up at Tom.

'No.' Willa pointed at Zain. 'It was him.'

Chapter Fourteen

Salma set aside her coffee and hurried to answer the door. Linda was on the step outside and Salma was suddenly aware that she hadn't yet showered or changed. She tightened the belt of her dressing gown.

'Hi, Linda. Please excuse the state of me. We're having a bit of a late start.' She beckoned her inside. 'Tea?'

'No, I won't stop for long.' Linda hovered just inside the door. 'I wanted to let you know that there's some trouble brewing on the Nextdoor app. People are talking about what happened to Willa yesterday. They're saying they feel unsafe.'

'Unsafe?' Salma shook her head. 'But it was an accident. She barely had a graze on her. Even the police agreed.'

Linda's face was grave. 'Salma, haven't you heard? Willa lost her baby yesterday.'

Salma's jaw dropped. By instinct, she reached for excuses. She wanted to tell Linda that she had seen Willa smoking and drinking but couldn't bring herself to do it. 'What are people saying?'

'They want you to go,' said Linda.

'Go? Where?'

Linda coloured. 'I don't know, but I wanted to warn you.' She smiled softly. 'I should go, but you will be okay, won't you, Salma?'

Salma was caught off guard by Linda's concern. 'I will. Thank you.' She closed the door behind her and slumped to the floor. Willa had lost her baby. Salma felt a complex knot of emotion: grief for Willa's loss, guilt for thinking she was being dramatic and, most of all, fear of the coming attack.

Chapter Fifteen

It happened three days later, on a Tuesday morning at precisely 5 a.m. Salma knew because she read the red digits on her alarm clock as soon as she jerked awake.

She shook Bil. 'There's someone downstairs.' She felt the heat roll off him as he sat up in bed, groggy at first but then instantly alert when he heard the battering sound. He was out of the room before she could protest. It happened all at once: a stampede of footsteps and the voices of angry men. Three burst into her room.

'Police! Get out of bed. Now!'

Salma's legs didn't move. One of the men – a hulk wearing protective gear – pulled the duvet off her. 'Get up and against the wall!' When she didn't listen, he yanked her out of bed. She spilled onto her knees, unable to move her feet in time. 'If you don't listen, we'll put you in cuffs,' he shouted.

Salma saw two, three, four men run up the stairs.

'Move,' said the hulk. When she didn't, he gave her a shove. 'Move!'

Salma stumbled onto the landing. Downstairs, she found Bil facedown against the floor. The baseball bat he kept for security was a few metres away.

'Do you have a garage?' said the man standing above Bil. He was taller than the hulk and also in protective gear. 'A basement? Storage of any kind?'

Bil raised his head but then pulled it low again. 'No. Just a shed. The key is on the kitchen rack.'

'Get up,' the man told him.

Salma flinched at the sound of a bang upstairs. By instinct, she moved towards it.

The hulk reached for his yellow taser. 'Don't move! Don't you move!'

'Why are you doing this?' cried Salma.

The taller man answered. 'We have reason to believe that your son has been supplying knives to under-eighteens.'

Bil looked up with disbelief. 'Knives? You must have the wrong house. My son would never—' A strange look dawned on his face. His voice changed, became low and more controlled. 'Officer, please tell your men to stay calm. My son will cooperate.'

There was a thud upstairs and Salma strained

for the sound of Zain's voice. 'Where's my son?' She felt a lick of panic. 'Bring me my son!'

'Salma, it's okay,' said Bil in a warning voice.

The taller officer, who she now knew was called Wilson, ushered them outside. Salma's nerves were jangling, stirring full-blown panic. She was so close to losing control, but then she heard a glorious sound.

'Mum, I'm okay!' Zain was led from the house.

Salma folded in relief. She tried to go to him but Bil held her back and weirdly tried to shield her from him. That's when she saw it: a dark patch in Zain's grey joggers, in between his legs. The sight filled her with desperate sorrow. What had they done to Zain to scare him that much?

'You're free to return to your home,' said Wilson as Zain was led to a car.

'Where are you taking my son?'

'We're driving him to the station.'

Salma saw the look on his face. 'You didn't find anything, did you?'

'We'll be in touch,' he said.

'You'll be in touch?' She scoffed with disbelief. 'That's it? You drag us out of bed at 5 a.m. and you tell me you'll be in *touch*?'

Bil touched her arm. 'Salma, come on. We need to go to the station.'

Wilson began to walk away. Salma moved to

follow him, but Bil tightened his grip. 'Someone told them,' he said quietly.

She turned to him. 'What?'

'Someone told the police about the box of knives from Jakoni's. Suli's nephew picked them up. Zain gave them to him.'

Salma froze. Suli's nephew was only seventeen. 'So they might have a case?'

Bil didn't answer. Salma's head buzzed with panic. From the corner of her eye, she saw a curtain twitch. She turned to see Willa at her window with a strange, satisfied look on her face.

Salma was hit with the answer. 'Bil, it was her.' She knew with impossible certainty that Willa was behind this. She pelted over to the window. 'Open the door,' she shouted.

Willa seemed to consider this, then shrugged as if it to say *why not?* A moment later, she appeared on her doorstep.

'Did you do this?' Salma's voice was shrill.

'I have no idea what you're talking about,' said Willa.

'The police raided our house! At 5 a.m. Willa, do you not understand what happens to boys like mine? He could have been killed.'

Willa's face softened a little.

'Was it you?' Salma repeated.

Willa shook her head and there was such

honesty in her sorrow, the air went out of Salma's fury. She covered her face with her hands. What was she *doing*? This woman had lost her baby and Salma hadn't even said she was sorry. When had she lost her common decency? She looked up at her now. 'I'm sorry about what happened, Willa. Please understand that it was an accident.' For a moment, she thought that Willa would listen, but instead she shut the door. A clean, cutting sound that severed a link once and for all.

Chapter Sixteen

Zain waited in the airless interview room. There were no windows and he had no idea how long he had been in there. His mind was spinning with images of this nightmare morning. Men folded over his bed, screaming in his face. The terror he had felt was deep and primal. He had cowered from them and to his great shame wet himself like a five-year-old.

At the station, they gave him a change of clothes, then asked him endless questions: Have you been supplying knives to minors? Why does a witness say they saw you? Do you use Tor? Do you own any bitcoins, cryptocurrency? What type? How much? How many knives have you sold?

Zain had tried to explain. 'The knives are from my dad's restaurant,' he told them. 'Dad's friend, Suli, said he would buy them. His nephew picked them up. He was just fooling around with the knives, pretending to be a ninja. I swear I told him off and resealed the box.'

But then the questions had got stranger: Have

you ever been to Pakistan? Why do you have a copy of *The Anarchist Cookbook*? What did you mean when you tweeted 'End the Monarchy'? What about 'Free Palestine'? Zain had always thought that people could see him for what he was – a computer coder and a nerd – but these questions ignored everything about him except the way he looked.

The door clanged open, making Zain tense. His interviewer, a wiry man called DS Buckley, tossed a file on the table. 'You're free to go.'

'Go?'

'We spoke to your dad's friend and your story checks out.'

Zain waited, expecting more: a parting word or apology, but there was nothing. Outside, his parents crowded him with hugs, but he pushed them off. At home, he escaped upstairs as soon as they got in. He felt ashamed when he saw that his sheets had been changed. He couldn't bring himself to touch the bed, so slumped in his chair instead.

Someone on their street had seen him handing over the knives. Had they known that *this* was the reason he'd been thrown out of college? He still remembered the shock when they found the knife in his locker. *It's not mine,* he had told them, but wouldn't tell them who it really belonged to.

He'd thought that Imran would do the decent thing and confess that the knife was his.

Zain had merely stored his friend's gym kit to save him a trip across campus. Instead, Imran said nothing and Zain was expelled from college under their zero tolerance policy. Now, that very same ghost had come back to haunt him.

He put his head in his hands and that's when he heard the sound – faint but familiar. He sprang up from the chair and darted downstairs. He hadn't imagined it. There was Molly in the hall-way, happily wagging her tail. Zain cried out and fell to his knees.

'Molly, oh my sweetheart.' He pulled her into his arms and looked up at his dad. 'How?'

'I stopped at the restaurant after my shift and saw that the window was smashed. The squatters were gone. They left Molly behind.'

Zain began to cry. 'Oh, Molly.' He ran a hand over her coat, checking for signs of injury. 'I promise I will never send you away again.' His tears landed softly in her fur. 'Dad,' he croaked. 'Thank you.'

'You're welcome, kid.' His dad ruffled his hair but then hurried away. Perhaps he, like Zain, needed a moment alone to wash off his distress.

Chapter Seventeen

Zain bent the pencil until it snapped in two. Since the raid last week, he found himself getting angry about simple things. A tangled wire or lost remote would fill him with a dark fury. The rage would build and make him want to scream. He had shouted once when his parents were out but felt guilty for scaring Molly. He didn't know what she had been through and blamed himself for her strange ducking motion when he tried to stroke her head. Had the squatters been cruel to her?

He set down the broken pencil and went to the balcony with his last cigarette. The flame wouldn't catch and once again stirred his rage.

'Zain?' said Jamie's voice.

Zain leaned out and saw him on the balcony like the first time they met. They hadn't spoken since their clash three weeks ago. *Are you dumb as well as deaf?* So much had happened since then.

'I've been texting you. We've got to upload our demo today.'

Zain casually lit his cigarette and leaned on the balcony wall.

Jamie grew agitated. 'Look, I've got to get to tutoring. If we don't do this now, we'll lose the rest of our funding.'

'You wanna talk? Let's talk.' Zain stubbed out his cigarette. He climbed onto the ledge and stepped around the central column onto Jamie's balcony. 'What shall we talk about? How your dad stole my dog? How he sent coppers to raid my house?'

'He didn't do that.'

'He did.'

'I know my dad, Zain. You're blaming him for something he didn't do. You're treating *me* like shit when I haven't done anything to you.'

'The fuck you haven't. I asked you for five hundred quid for Molly and you pulled rank on me.'

'So you act like *this?*'

'What are you going to do about it?'

Jamie blinked nervously.

Normally, Zain found this tic endearing, but today it enraged him. He blinked in the same way, cruelly mimicking Jamie. 'What is little old Jamie gonna do about it?' The stress of the past few weeks pulsed through his body. He shoved Jamie's shoulder.

'Zain, don't do this.'

He pushed him again. 'Do what?'

Jamie took a step back. 'Come on, man. I've got to get to my tutoring.'

The pathetic note in Jamie's voice made Zain want to lash out more. 'Jesus Christ. Stop being such a pussy. Stand up to me.' Zain pushed him again. 'Stand up to me.'

This time, Jamie pushed back.

'That's it!' Zain swiped at Jamie's ear. He barely touched him but made him flinch. 'Come on.' Zain pushed his chest. 'Come *on*.'

Jamie put his fists up and Zain laughed in cruel approval, even as he felt something precious slipping away from him.

Chapter Eighteen

Salma looked around the empty restaurant, now freshly painted, and felt a new lightness in her bones. Tomorrow, a keen buyer was coming to see it, and she and Bil were feeling positive. As they locked up to leave, Salma heard her phone ring and groped for it in her bag.

'Salma? It's Linda.' Her neighbour spoke in gasps as if she was treading water. 'You have to come home.'

'Linda? What's wrong?'

'I can't hear you, Salma, but please come home. Now.'

Salma tuned out her panic. 'Is it Zain?' She heard Linda swallow, and then the three short beeps of a lost signal. 'We have to go,' she told Bil.

They bolted from the building, down the street to their car. Bil drove too fast, changing lanes with skill that Salma had never seen. When they reached Hampton, her blood turned to ice. Three police cars and an ambulance were outside her house. When she got out, however, she realised that they were parked next door.

Salma called for Zain as they hurried into the house. She searched the kitchen and living room while Bil went upstairs. The garden door was unlocked but Zain wasn't outside. She ran upstairs after Bil. Zain's bedroom door was open but the room was empty. There were voices in Tom's garden and Bil was out on the balcony. When he looked at her, his eyes were strange and glassy. Salma joined him but it took her a while to see through the cluster of police and paramedics. Then they moved away, and Salma screamed.

The figure on the grass was clear: Zain, unmoving, his skull braced by large red blocks. The purple of his hoodie against the dark green formed the colours of Wimbledon, a fact that Salma took on even as her mind unhinged itself. The sound she made wasn't shrill like a scream but a deep wail. Bil pelted out of the room. Seconds later, he appeared in their garden and moved through the broken fence into Tom's. He shouted up to Salma.

'He's breathing!'

Salma grew shaky with relief. She stumbled downstairs and into Tom's garden. The paramedics spoke quietly, but Salma caught an appalling pair of words: *spinal injury*. They lifted Zain onto a yellow stretcher and steered him into the house. Salma spotted Tom in his kitchen window, surrounded by four officers. Questions fired in her head: *Why is Zain in Tom's garden? Did he fall? Did he lose his footing or …?*

Bil and Salma followed the paramedics. The ambulance was leaving already and they hurried to their car. Salma snapped at Bil for falling too far behind and he went past the speed limit to try to keep up. Her small unkindness made Salma ache with shame. How cruel that in a crisis, her instinct was to turn on him. Bil touched her knee briefly, granting forgiveness before she even asked for it.

In the hospital, they sat for hours in A & E. When the news came, she received it with a strange calm, as if collapsing in the corridor might bother the doctor. Zain was in a coma, he said. The trauma to his brain was severe and, while most patients got better within a few weeks, they could not say more at this stage.

It was only after the doctor left that Salma's legs buckled beneath her. The tears came in low, pathetic sobs. She wept for a long time but Bil did not comfort her. In all their time together, Bil had been strong, cheerful and kind, but now he just stood there, wordless and pale. Salma dug her nails into his palm, but he didn't seem to feel it, or her, or *anything*.

PART II

Chapter Nineteen

Five months later

Tom sat in the dock, surrounded by bulletproof plastic. He was sweating and prayed that it wouldn't show through his suit. He wanted to look calm even though his heart was hammering. Judge Braithwaite sat across the courtroom, directly opposite Tom. He wore a deep red gown and horsehair wig and spoke in a deep baritone.

Tom's barrister, Julian Hughes, sat on the left side of the courtroom, closest to the jury. He was in his late forties and wore a black silk gown over a designer suit. The prosecutor, Charlotte Ashman, was in her late fifties and also wore a black silk gown. She fixed her striking grey eyes on the jury and stood to make her opening speech.

'Members of the jury, we have all heard that appearances can be deceiving. It's an old saying, a cliché, but like many clichés, it holds some truth. On first glance, the defendant, Tom Hutton, seems respectable. Until recently, he held down a job at an advertising agency. He is a husband and father and he takes an active role in the community. In May of this year, however, Mr Hutton started a campaign of hate against his neighbours, which ended in the attempted murder of Zain Khatun.

'Zain was only eighteen years old when he was found in Tom Hutton's garden with grave injuries caused by a fall from height. Zain was taken to hospital but fell into a coma. Five months later, he remains in a vegetative state. So what happened that day?

'Tom Hutton says he came home at 5.50 p.m. that evening. He says that he found Zain lying in the garden. He says that he has no idea how Zain got there and that he called an ambulance straight away. It is our case that Tom Hutton knows exactly what happened; that he in fact *pushed* Zain from a third-storey balcony, knowing full well that this could cause his death. Here are four facts of the case.

'One: a neighbour saw a man matching Tom's description on the balcony at 5.50 p.m., five minutes before he called the ambulance.

'Two: Tom says he came home at 5.50 p.m. This means that either the man on the balcony and Tom were in the house at the same time and the man escaped without Tom noticing or, more likely, the other man doesn't exist and *Tom* was the man on the balcony.

'Three: leading up to the attack, Tom started a racially charged campaign against the Khatun family. You will hear how his own son, Jamie, hid his friendship with Zain, the victim.

'Four: on a prior occasion, Tom had threatened to hurt Zain. It is our case that when Tom came home that day to find Zain in his house, he reacted violently.'

Charlotte pointed at the dock. 'If Tom claimed self-defence, or said that he mistook Zain for an intruder, we might have understood, but he denies he was there at all. According to Tom, a stranger snuck into his home, pushed Zain, then escaped just in time for Tom to arrive and discover Zain on his lawn. There is no evidence to support this and so we have to rely on the facts.

'We *know* that Tom Hutton repeatedly clashed with his neighbours. This is a central part of the puzzle so this is where I'll start – with Zain's mother because it's Tom's relationship with her that led to his campaign: verbal abuse that became physical and ultimately all but lethal. If you are convinced of these facts, then we ask that you find Tom Hutton guilty of attempted murder.'

Chapter Twenty

Salma stood in the witness box and reminded herself to breathe. The prosecutor, Charlotte Ashman, aimed to do two things: to show that Tom was aggressive and to plant the seed that this was racially motivated. She expertly guided Salma through the events that led them here: the banner, the spray paint, the tweet about 'tolerant Britain', Tom getting fired, the squatters who took Molly, Willa's miscarriage and, finally, the police raid. Together, they made a strong basis for the case, but soon it was time to face the defence.

Julian Hughes, the defence barrister, fixed his stare on Salma. 'Mrs Khatun, do you have an issue with white people?'

Salma was caught by surprise. She cleared her throat and answered, 'No.'

'So you have never made negative public remarks about white people? White *women* in particular?'

'No.'

'Interesting.' Julian gestured towards the TV screens which displayed a tweet.

WW genuinely think they rule the world and that
we're all just here to serve them.

'The username @eastlondonteacher – is that you?'
Salma felt a jolt of dread. 'Yes.'
'Can I ask, what does WW mean?'
Heat rose in her cheeks. 'White women,' she
admitted.
Julian raised his brows in a stagey manner.
'So that sentence in full reads, "White women
genuinely think they rule the world and that
we're all just here to serve them." Is that
correct?'
Salma could feel the sharp focus of the jury.
'Yes.'
Another tweet was shown on-screen.

WW are unbelievable.

This one was attached to a video and Salma
wished that they would play it for much-needed
background. It showed a middle-aged white
woman preventing a Latino man from entering
his own building because she did not believe that
he lived there.
Another tweet came up.

WW's tears are lethal.

This was also attached to a video that wasn't played for the jury. This one was filmed by a bird-watcher who was verbally abused in Central Park, New York, after asking a woman to put her dog on a leash. The woman had called the police and claimed she had been threatened by an *African American* man. Salma had listened to the faked tremble of the woman's voice and dashed off the tweet without thinking.

Julian adjusted his glasses. 'I want to show you a sample of tweets from Tom's wife, who is indeed a white woman.'

Just had the most amazing time with my bestie.

This was attached to a picture of Willa and a pretty Asian woman holding cocktails to the camera. Salma made a cynical sound that was louder than she had intended.

Women of colour need our support.

Let's keep our feminism intersectional please. #translivesmatter

Representation matters. #OscarsSoWhite

Julian turned to Salma. 'Does this look like some-one who is racist?'

'Willa's not the one who hurt my son.'

'Do you think a woman like that would stay married to a racist?'

'I think you would be surprised what people condone behind closed doors.'

'If that's true and you're already comfortable vilifying white women publicly, what do you say behind closed doors?'

'I'm not the one on trial.'

'No, but we do need to look at your reasons for accusing Tom, don't we? Tell me, have your neighbours ever called you a racist slur?'

Salma thought about this. 'No, but they have said "these people". Like "these people don't know how lucky they are".'

'How do you know they weren't talking about teachers or chefs or any number of things? Why assume the worst? Could it be that in your cru-sade against white women, you saw things that simply weren't there?'

'No.'

Julian changed direction. 'Mrs Khatun, isn't it true that you moved to Hampton to give your son a better life?'

'Yes.'

'Was he in some sort of trouble?'

Salma sensed a trap. 'No.'

'But he *was* expelled from college?'

'Yes.' Salma tried to sound neutral. 'A banned item was found in his locker.'

'What sort of item?'

'A knife.' Salma felt the jury tense. 'It wasn't his. He was storing a friend's gym kit.'

'Well, isn't that convenient,' said Julian. 'And there were other signs of trouble, weren't there? He got into fights?'

'One fight.'

'But enough to give him a bloody nose?'

'Yes,' Salma admitted.

'With whom did he fight?'

'He wouldn't say.'

'But it was clear that someone wanted to hurt your son?'

So *this* is what Julian was trying to do; to shift the blame from Tom.

'Mrs Khatun, isn't that why you moved home?'

'We wanted to give him a better life. Good kids can turn bad in a place like that.'

Julian pounced on this. 'Good kids can turn bad,' he said with relish. 'And that's what happened to your son, isn't it?'

'No, but it could have.'

'Just so we're clear: your son is found with a knife. Soon after, he is attacked but you don't know by whom. You move a mere two miles away with the goal of keeping him safe, and not long after, someone attacks him again. Is that correct?'

'They're not the ones who pushed Zain. They don't even know where we live.'

'You still work at the same school, no? Could they have followed you home?'

'That's not what happened.'

'The fact is, there are people who wanted to hurt your son and you thought the threat was so real that you moved home, is that not correct?'

'We moved for several reasons. Because we wanted a better life.'

'Because "good kids can turn bad"! Well, Mrs Khatun, yours got mixed up in some very nasty business and you automatically blamed your white neighbour. Isn't that true?'

'No. You're twisting things.'

'That's not true, is it, Mrs Khatun?'

She couldn't unpick the question to answer the right way. *No, it's not true* that I'm blaming my neighbour, but *yes, it is true* that you're twisting things.

Julian looked at her with a mix of scorn and pity. 'I think we'll leave it there,' he said.

Salma left the witness box. Outside, she

crumpled into Bil's arms and cried exhausted tears. She had thought that this day would bring relief. Instead, she felt robbed of her chance at justice.

Chapter Twenty-One

Salma sat in the public gallery and watched the woman in the witness box. Josephine Steinem had thick grey hair styled in a Sixties flip and wore royal blue trousers and a crimson jacket. The jury had spent the last two days listening to forensic evidence and this was a welcome change.

'Ms Steinem,' the prosecutor, Charlotte, was saying, 'do you remember what you were you doing at 5.50 p.m. on the day of the incident?'

'Yes. I was watching a quiz show with my husband. The adverts come on at 5.50 p.m. and I popped upstairs for a blanket. That's when I saw Tom.'

'Where was he?'

'On his balcony, directly opposite mine.'

'You would have been over twenty metres away. Are you sure that it was Tom Hutton you saw?'

'I'm certain. He had the same build and the same colour hair.'

'Thank you, Ms Steinem.'

Salma felt a shoot of hope. If this calm and credible woman was sure that she had seen Tom, surely he couldn't deny it?

The defence barrister, Julian, stood now to cross-examine Josephine. 'Ms Steinem, do you wear glasses?'

'No. I've never needed them.'

'I notice that you're squinting at the jury. Do you have problems with your eyesight?'

She seemed insulted. 'No. My sight is perfectly fine.'

'In that case, would you mind pointing out Tom Hutton in the dock?'

She tutted and before Charlotte could stop her, she pointed at Tom in the dock.

'Why do you think that's Tom?' asked Julian.

'Because he's less than ten metres away from me,' she said impatiently. 'Because I know what he looks like. And because he's wearing his orange cap.'

'I see.' Julian turned towards the dock. 'Could the gentleman in the orange cap please stand up?'

For a moment, no one moved. Then Tom stood up and took off his cap. To Josephine's shock, it wasn't Tom at all. This man was of a similar build but with different coloured hair – almost blond to Tom's dark brown – and completely different features.

'Will the defendant, Tom Hutton, please stand?' said Julian.

This time, Tom stood up. He was at the opposite end of the dock, in clear sight of the witness box.

Julian swallowed a smile. 'I have no more questions, My Lord.'

Chapter Twenty-Two

Salma tensed as she watched Tom walk to the witness box. In his navy suit, he looked like a perfect gentleman. Sure enough, as he took the oath, his voice dropped to a respectful tone with none of his usual bravado. Tom was the primary witness for the defence and Julian stood to question him first.

'Mr Hutton, what was your first impression of your neighbours?'

'They seemed nice,' said Tom. 'Educated. Professional. A bit reserved but that's normal at first.'

'When was the first time there was a problem between your families?'

Tom thought about this. 'When I asked if they could try not to park in front of our house. Salma got passive aggressive and said, "Oh, I didn't realise there was *designated* parking".' He said the words tartly – nothing like Salma's actual tone. 'I didn't want to tell her that it was bad manners, so I let it go.'

'I see.' Julian led Tom through the many clashes that followed. He spent a whole hour on Tom's firing and Willa's miscarriage to show how much their lives had been damaged. 'Mr Hutton, just so we're clear, did you steal Mrs Khatun's dog?'

'No, sir.'

'Did you tell someone else to steal her dog?'

'No, sir.'

'Did you report her son for selling knives?'

'No, sir.'

'And did you paint her window?'

Tom hung his head. 'Yes, I did do that, sir.'

Salma jolted in surprise. Finally, the truth.

'Why?' asked Julian.

'I was annoyed that they put up a banner when it's not allowed.'

'Did you have a problem with the message? I believe it said "Black Lives Matter". Did you disagree?'

'Of course not. It could have said Blue Lives Matter. I just wanted them to understand that it wasn't allowed.'

'Why not talk to them?'

Tom grimaced. 'I thought that making it look like local kids would make them feel more comfortable. If your neighbours complain about you, you'll never feel at home. If it's just local kids, it doesn't feel so personal. I honestly wanted them to feel safe here. I just did it in a clumsy way and for that I am truly sorry.'

Salma was almost convinced by this display of regret. Tom was so earnest, it was hard not to believe him.

Julian continued. 'Did Mrs Khatun talk to you about your wife's miscarriage? Did she explain or offer you an apology?'

Tom took a moment to compose himself. It was clear to the jury that here was a father still grieving. 'No,' he said softly. 'We were left to mourn our child alone.'

'And how did that make you feel?'

'Devastated. Angry.'

'Enough to seek revenge?'

'No, sir. I live by the rules. It's why I reacted so strongly to the banner in the first place.'

Salma flushed. This respectful man was nothing like the one she knew, but the jury couldn't see that.

'Did you have any contact with Zain after the day of your wife's miscarriage?'

'No, sir.'

'What went through your mind when you found him lying in your garden?'

'I didn't think. My training as a first aider kicked in.'

'Did you go to the hospital with him?'

'No. The police took me to the station and the next thing I know I'm being arrested for attempted murder. All because I painted a window.'

Chapter Twenty-Three

Charlotte Ashman fixed her gaze on Tom. 'Mr Hutton, you said that banners are not allowed on your street. According to what rule?'

Tom didn't hesitate. 'Section 24 of Hampton's housing regulations.'

'Is placing a banner in your window against the law?'

'No.'

'Do you know what *is* against the law? Painting a neighbour's window.'

Salma felt a pang of satisfaction when she saw Tom's face. It was clear that he didn't know what to say.

'I regret that deeply,' he said finally. 'I should have spoken to Salma directly.'

'Have any of your other neighbours put up banners from time to time?'

'Sometimes.'

'Have you ever knocked out those banners?'

'I can't recall but I may have.'

'We looked at other videos from Hampton's Facebook page. Do you know what we found?'

Charlotte motioned at the TV. Three separate houses were shown on-screen, all displaying the St George's Cross – one on the front door, another in a plant pot and a third hanging limply from a pole. 'These pictures show houses on your street, taken last year. Did you remove any of those flags or banners?'

Tom cleared his throat. 'That's different. It was during the football.'

'But Hampton's regulations say that you can't display any banners at all. You felt so strongly about this that you were willing to break the law. But you left these alone?'

'As I said, the football was on. It would be petty to force people to take them down.'

'So it wasn't *all* banners you had a problem with? Just ones that said *Black Lives Matter?*'

Tom grew impatient. 'Look, I would understand if Salma were Black, or had Black family, but she's not, so what was she trying to prove?'

'So you *did* have a problem with the message of the banner. If it was a St George's Cross, you would have left it alone, yes?'

'No,' he said testily. 'The people who know me, know me. This isn't what you say it is.'

'Is that why your employers fired you? Because they *know* you? Remind me, Mr Hutton, why *did* they fire you?'

'They saw a video of me and Salma arguing and they didn't like it.'

'This is the video recorded by the victim, Zain Khatun?'

'Yes.'

'What happens in the video that your employers felt they had to fire you?'

'I don't remember exactly.'

'Well, why don't we jog your memory?' Charlotte turned to the TV.

The screen showed Tom looming over Salma. 'And you call *me* intolerant?' he was saying. 'If I was intolerant, I'd tell your husband not to park in front of our house and I'd tell you to shut up that fucking dog of yours.' He pointed a finger in her face. 'I'd tell you to fix that fucking fence. And I'd tell you to keep your windows closed so you don't stink up our clothes with your cooking!' Murmurs of shock rose in the courtroom. A juror stared at the screen open-mouthed. Another visibly squirmed. Salma now understood why Charlotte hadn't shown the video earlier in the trial. She wanted the jury to see the respectable face of Tom first.

'"Stink,"' said Charlotte. The word seemed to echo. 'What did you mean by that?'

Tom's face grew pink. 'Look, people think I meant curry, but I meant food *in general*. Salma just took everything the wrong way. When you move to a new area, you should try to get along, not make a big deal of your differences, try to fit in.'

'Especially if you're not white?'

'That isn't … Stop making this into something it's not.'

'Mr Hutton, isn't it true that your son, Jamie, hid his friendship with Zain from you?'

Tom didn't answer.

'On the evening of the incident, Jamie let Zain work in his room while he went tutoring. You were not aware of this, so when you came home to find Zain in your house, you lost your temper, isn't that right?'

'No, I didn't even go upstairs.'

'Why did you push him, Mr Hutton?'

'I didn't.'

'Was he giving you lip? Getting in your face?'

'No.'

'But you *did* threaten him just weeks earlier with "you'll see what I can do"?'

'No.'

'You didn't say that?'

'I did, but—'

'So you did threaten him?'

'It wasn't a threat. I was just pretending.'

'Were you pretending when you pushed him?'

'I didn't push him!'

'Well, then, can you explain this?'

An audio clip began to play over the courtroom speakers. With cold horror, Salma realised that it was Tom's phone call to the emergency services.

Yes, he's breathing. Tom's voice sounded panicked. *You've got to hurry. Please. Okay. Okay, I'll stay on the line.* And then, in a faint whimper: *I didn't mean it. Oh, God, I didn't mean it.*

Charlotte replayed the last section. 'What didn't you mean, Mr Hutton?'

Tom's face changed, now a mask of sorrow. 'All of it,' he said finally. 'The things I said to his family. The way I acted.'

Charlotte frowned. 'That would be a very odd choice of words and an odd time to apologise.'

Tom took a shaky breath. 'There was something I read about the Stephen Lawrence case years ago. The woman who found him held him and she said, "you are loved". I always thought that was such a kind thing to say. She didn't lie and say "you'll be okay". She said "you are loved" and I thought that if I was in that situation, I would want someone to be kind to me. I was trying to make Zain feel safe in case ...' Tom trailed off and Salma was amazed to see tears in his eyes.

'In case he died?' said Charlotte bluntly.

'Yes.'

'He didn't die, Mr Hutton, but he can't speak or move or tell the truth and the least he deserves is the truth from you, so tell us: you pushed him, didn't you?'

'It wasn't me.'

'Then who?'

For a moment, it seemed like he would give an answer. But then he hung his head and said, 'I don't know.'

Chapter Twenty-Four

Salma and Bil held hands as they left the court-house. Journalists crowded around them and a microphone grazed her cheek. Bil's grip grew tight as he led her through the mass.

'Excuse me,' he said, using his free hand to keep them away. One journalist shouted questions in Salma's face. Bil pressed against the man's chest. 'Please don't shout at my wife.' When he didn't listen, Bil gave him a shove. The man stumbled and lost his footing. Bil ignored him and whisked Salma to their car. He locked the doors and jammed the key in the ignition. 'Fucking leeches.'

'You shouldn't have shoved that guy,' said Salma. 'What if he sues us?'

Bil gripped the steering wheel. 'What did you want me to do?'

'Nothing.'

'Nothing,' he mimicked meanly. 'Why? So you can call me an Uncle Tom?'

Salma was shocked by the venom in his voice. 'Bil, I have *never* said that about you.'

'So calling me "a good immigrant" wasn't a jibe?'

She winced. 'Bil—'

He turned the ignition on and zoomed out of the car park.

'Bil,' she tried again. She knew he was stressed, but he had never shut her out like this. In the silence, Salma felt her anger build. When they reached the hospital, Bil barely looked at her.

'I don't think I'll come up tonight.'

Salma checked her watch. 'You still have time before your shift.'

'Barely.'

'You have fifteen minutes. That's enough time to say hi.'

'It's fine. I'd rather get going.'

'Bil—'

'Just *go*,' he snapped, making her flinch.

She waited to see if he would apologise. 'Fine,' she said coldly. She got out and slammed the door. She was a car length away when the window whirred behind her.

'Salma.'

She stopped but didn't face him.

'Do you think it's true?'

She turned. 'What's true?'

'That Tom said what he said because he thought that Zain might die?'

Salma felt herself sway. 'I don't know.'

'I want it to be true. I want to know that Tom was kind to our son.' He looked at her with desperation. 'Because what if they're the last words he ever hears?'

'Bil, don't.' She reached for him but he waved her back.

'I can't, Salma. I just … I can't see him today.'

'Okay,' she said gently.

'You give my boy a kiss for me.' Bil's voice cracked.

Salma nodded, then turned and headed inside, giving him space to break down.

Chapter Twenty-Five

Salma looked on as Jamie took his place in the witness box. She felt a sense of tenderness even though he was there in Tom's defence. He looked small and scared, and squinted every time he was asked a question. It was clear that it took all of his focus to hear what the defence barrister was saying.

'What was Zain doing in your house that day?' asked Julian.

'He came over to work on Grapevine, our app,' said Jamie.

'Were you in the house when Zain fell?'

'No. I tutor at deafPLUS at five on Fridays. I told Zain to work on my computer. It's faster and we were on a deadline. I told him I'd be back in an hour or so.'

'Did you lock the door when you left?'

'No. Zain was home so I didn't think I had to.'

'Do you have any security at home? Anything to alert you to an intruder?'

'No. Just Lola, our dog, but she comes to deaf-PLUS with me.'

'So anyone could have walked in?'

Jamie grimaced. 'Yes.'

'Before he fell, did Zain seem stressed about anything?'

Salma watched on anxiously. Before the incident, Zain had indeed seemed angry. She and Bil had even discussed therapy.

Jamie wiped a palm on his trousers. 'A few weeks before he fell, Zain asked me for five hundred pounds. He said it was a reward for his missing dog, but I felt like it was something else. He seemed desperate and got nasty when I said no.'

'Nasty? In what way?'

'He started shouting at me. When I didn't react, he said, "Are you dumb as well as deaf?"'

Salma stared at Jamie. That couldn't possibly be true. The Zain she knew stood up for vulnerable people.

Jamie continued. 'But Zain wasn't normally like that, which made me think that the money wasn't for his dog. It made me think there was something else going on.'

'Did he give you any sign what that might be?'

Jamie fiddled with his tie. 'No, but I saw him using a gambling app and wondered if it was that.'

Salma felt pressure in her chest. Had Zain got into trouble that he couldn't escape?

'Do you know if Zain borrowed money off

someone else?' asked Julian. 'Someone who might have wanted it back?'

'No.'

'Okay, here are some things we do know: Zain needed money – enough to turn him nasty. We know he was stressed about not having this money. And we know that the door to your house was unlocked. Someone may have come in and hurt him. Do you think this was your father?'

'No. Dad would never go for someone smaller than him.'

'Have you ever seen your father be violent?'

'No.'

'Have you ever heard him make a racist remark?'

'No.'

'How certain are you that your father is innocent?'

'One hundred per cent,' said Jamie.

Chapter Twenty-Six

Salma felt coiled with tension as Charlotte stood up to question Jamie. He was the last witness of the trial and this was their final chance at justice.

'Jamie, you said that Zain used a gambling app.' Charlotte nodded at the TV screen. 'Was it this?'

Jamie squinted at the blue and white logo. 'Yes. I saw him losing money on it.'

'This,' she said slowly, 'is an app called CoinPace. It allows users to play with cryptocurrency in a safe way with no risk to any real money. It is *not* a gambling app.' Her voice was sharp and full of accusation. 'What we *know* is that Zain didn't *need* money. He wanted it to rescue his dog. He wasn't a gambling addict. There was no reason for a stranger to harm him, or for him to harm himself. So we come back to your father, Tom Hutton, who you say has never been violent or racist.' Charlotte glared at him. 'Tell me, how did Zain enter your room on the day of his fall?'

Jamie wiped his upper lip. 'He came from his balcony to mine.'

Charlotte pointed at the TV, which showed

a picture of the brick column that stuck out between the two balconies. 'To get from his room to yours, he needs to step around this column. Why did he use such a dangerous passage?'

'It was easier.'

'No, Jamie. It was easier for him to use the front door.'

Jamie squirmed. 'We used it because Dad didn't know we were working together.'

'You hid it from him?'

'Yes.'

'Why?'

'He wanted me to stay away from Zain. He said he was bad news.'

'Why? What gave him that idea?'

'I don't know. He was being paranoid.'

'Your father's a bully, isn't he?'

'No.'

'If that's true, then you won't mind telling us what happened with your friend, David Adeleye, will you?'

Jamie froze. With frantic eyes, he scanned the dock for his father.

'Will you tell us about the night that David Adeleye came to your house?' asked Charlotte.

Jamie's lips moved, soundlessly at first. 'It was years ago now,' he said. 'David came to a sleepover.'

'Go on,' Charlotte pressed.

Jamie spoke with hesitation. 'There were seven of us in my room. We were wrestling and having a laugh. Someone said we should arm wrestle. The bed was too soft so we went downstairs. Mum was out, so Dad was keeping an eye on us. He saw what we were doing and had a laugh with us.'

'And then?'

'Well, David kept winning and Dad said it wasn't fair because he was naturally stronger than the rest of us.'

'Why did your dad think that?'

Jamie looked at the floor. 'Because David was Black.'

Noise rose in the courtroom.

'And then?'

'Dad wanted to make it fair so he went to the shed and he got these weights that he uses for running. He tied them around David's wrist to put extra pressure on him.'

The jury watched in astonishment.

'David was embarrassed and said he didn't want to play, but Dad told him he was chickening out because now things were fair. David still won and Dad got annoyed. He was looking around for something else to put on his arm. I told him to leave it, but he didn't want to. He said *he* would wrestle with David.'

'How old was David?'

Jamie swallowed. 'Twelve.'

'What happened?'

'It was an accident.'

'What happened, Jamie?'

'Dad didn't know how strong he was.'

'What happened?'

'He broke David's arm.'

The courtroom grew still and Charlotte let the silence hang. She turned to the judge. 'I have no further questions, My Lord.'

Chapter Twenty-Seven

It was a bright morning but the hospital lights were on full blast. This was one of the many things that Salma hated here. There was no slow advance from day to night. It was full-beam lights, then sudden dark at the click of a switch. Salma took Zain's hand. It was cold and his nails were blue. She held them to her mouth and blew gently to warm them. In that moment, with her own icy hand around his, she felt so utterly powerless. She tucked his hand beneath the blanket and tried to calm her jitters. Yesterday, the barristers had given their closing arguments and soon they would have a verdict.

To distract herself, she picked up an old newspaper and leafed through the pages. On page eight, she paused and took a closer look at a grainy photo. She recognised the boy. Thin hair, narrow nose, bad teeth. It was the squatter, Rich.

Teen found dead in Ilford stairwell

Salma felt a pang of shock. Quickly, she scanned the first paragraph.

The body of an 18-year-old male was found in the stairwell of a disused building in Ilford on Tuesday morning. The building, part of Abbey Estate, was evacuated for demolition in March 2019. But it has stood abandoned in the years since. It has become a magnet for drug users, with two reported stabbings. The dead man, identified as Richard Fremont, was found in the early hours by an outreach team from St Mungo's, a homelessness charity. Fremont was pronounced dead at the scene. His death was said to have been caused by a drug overdose.

Salma had once hated this boy but now she only felt sad. What had gone wrong in his life to bring him to such a tragic end? She read on, but her phone cut in before she could finish. She turned pale as she listened. The jury had a verdict.

Chapter Twenty-Eight

Salma emptied her pockets onto a circular metal plate: a dusty hairband, a crumpled receipt and a mint that had lost its wrapper. She passed through the metal detectors and waited for Bil on the other side. He had taken the day off and she was glad to have him by her side. Up in the public gallery, she spotted Willa in the back row, sitting next to Jamie. Salma and Bil took their own seats at the front.

'I believe we have a verdict, jury, please,' said Judge Braithwaite.

'Will the defendant please stand?' asked the clerk.

Tom stood and fastened the button of his suit jacket.

'Mr Foreman, have the jury reached a verdict upon which you are all agreed?'

A middle-aged man stood up. He was sweating despite the chill and sounded nervous when he answered. 'Yes.'

Salma saw the man glance at Tom, but couldn't tell what it meant.

'On count one, do you find the defendant guilty or not guilty of attempted murder?'

Salma leaned forward and waited for the man to speak. The thought of Tom being free made her sick. If that happened, she would sneak into his house one night and pick up his biggest knife and sink it into his son. *You took my child, so I'll take yours.*

It chilled her to realise that Tom had already lost one. Had he had the very same thought? *You took my child, so I'll take yours.*

Salma glared at the foreman, wanting to slap the words out of him. Finally, he spoke.

'Guilty.'

'You find the defendant guilty and that is the verdict of you all?'

'Yes.'

The word was like a pendulum swinging in her brain. *Guilty. Guilty. Guilty.* She sagged against Bil, weak with gratitude. He pulled her into his arms and she felt the breath in his chest, shaky with his own relief.

'Mr Hutton, you will be remanded in custody until sentencing,' the judge was saying. 'Thank you, members of the jury.'

Salma was overwhelmed. These twelve strangers had finally given her justice. Their support filled her with something close to joy. She stood and reached for Bil's hand. They didn't need to stay here any longer. They could leave. They could bring Zain home and start to rebuild their lives as Tom and Willa's fell apart. She realised how much strain she had felt all these months. The pressure seemed to bulge in the walls and infect the air around her. Now, the poison was gone and Salma could breathe once more.

PART III

Chapter Twenty-Nine

Five months later

Salma and Bil sat in the garden in the fading light.
The doors were open wide so that they could hear
the monitor. Zain was newly home, lying in the
living room, and they were careful not to leave
him alone. He still hadn't opened his eyes but
there were signs of improvement. Sometimes, his
eyelids would flutter and his breathing would
change rhythm. The doctors were still hopeful
and Salma took comfort from that.

Molly walked out to the garden and looked at
Bil expectantly.

Salma and Bil laughed. 'I'll walk her tonight,'
she said. 'I need to decompress.'

Bil glanced towards the living room. 'Can
I jump in the shower first? I'll be quick.' He
headed upstairs, already unbuttoning his shirt.

A moment later, the light went on in their
bedroom. Salma watched Bil's silhouette against
the curtain as he went through his routine. She
smiled when he leaned towards the mirror to
inspect a grey hair.

She heard a bark behind her, and groaned when she realised that Molly had escaped into next door's garden. Salma bent by the loose plank and called for her to come back. She scanned the garden but couldn't see any sign of her. After a few minutes, Salma squeezed through herself. She stayed low and called out quietly. The last thing she wanted was to be caught in Willa's garden.

'Molly,' she whispered. 'Come on, girl.' She heard her behind the shed. 'Molly, come on.' Salma crept forwards but froze when a light came on in the kitchen. She turned and saw Willa leaning over a kitchen counter. Salma wasn't sure if she should stand and wave to make it clear what she was doing, or try to get back undetected. She decided on the second option and crept towards the shed.

'Come *on*, girl.' She gripped Molly's collar and led her towards the fence, praying that she wouldn't bark. She steered her back through the gap.

As Salma followed, a glint caught her eye. It was a strip of gold wedged between the two panels that ran beneath the fence. She leaned closer to inspect it, then slid her fingers between the panels and tried to wiggle it free. It was stuck and she moved it back and forth to try to release it. Finally, it popped free and up onto the grass.

Salma's blood turned to ice when she saw what it was. An old Nokia phone with two stickers on the back: a marijuana leaf and a golden skull and crossbones. She knew that phone. Its owner had been Rich, the squatter. Dread rose inside her as she tried to make sense of this. Had Rich dropped his phone on the day he stole Molly?

No, because Salma saw him with the phone *after* that. He must have come back to . . . what? Steal Molly again? An awful thought came to her: could Zain have seen Rich taking Molly? He would have tried to stop him. Was it *Rich* who had hurt Zain that day?

She snatched up the phone and flipped it open. The screen was blank. She pressed the 'on' button a few times. To her surprise, the phone turned on. Molly barked at it and Salma pulled her close to quieten her. Then, with clumsy fingers, she opened the text messages on the old phone. There was only one.

Tom's gone and Jamie just left. Give it half an hour to be safe.

Salma stared at the message. *Tom's gone and Jamie just left* – sent on the day Zain fell. She looked up at Willa in the kitchen and was hit with a dreadful understanding. *Willa* had sent that message. *Willa* had sent Rich to the house.

You took my child, so I'll take yours.

Salma rocked back on her heels and hit the ground with a jolt. She scrambled away from the fence. Her fingers trembled as she handled the phone. She pressed the green button to call the sender and held the phone to her ear. The sweat on her skin grew cool, making her shiver. She held her breath as the phone made clicking sounds in her ear. At first, she didn't think it would work, but then she heard the ringing.

Willa turned off the kitchen tap and hurried out of view. Salma could hear her phone ring from here. A moment later, Willa came back into view. In her hands she carried a microwave meal, the steam rising off in waves. She dropped it onto the counter and at that very second, the phone call was answered.

'Hello?'

The voice was like a shotgun, making the air vibrate. Horror churned inside her as she looked up at the second storey.

'Bil?' The word was soft and breathless.

His silhouette paused in the window, phone pressed to his ear. He ripped apart the curtains and their eyes met like a bolt of lightning. Every nerve in her body was lit up with panic. The wild look on his face was shocking and when he bolted out of the room, Salma felt like she had to move. She ran inside the house with Molly at her heels. She spun around in a panic as Bil barged into the living room.

'Salma,' Bil said calmly. 'Give me the phone.'

She gripped it tightly. 'Bil, what is this?'

'Give me the phone.'

Salma darted to Zain's bed. 'Bil.' Her voice shook. 'What's happening?'

'Give me the phone and we'll talk.' He stepped towards her with his hands up.

She moved away from him, around to other side of the bed.

His voice grew hard. 'Come on, Salma. Just give me the fucking phone.' He lunged at her and she leapt away with a short, sharp yelp.

'Bil, stop it!' She backed into the kitchen, her voice high with panic.

He slapped the railing and followed her. 'Give me the phone, Salma.' He lunged again and Salma lost her grip on the phone. It flew across the floor and skidded beneath the fridge.

Bil growled with anger. He bent by the fridge and slid his fingers underneath. 'For fuck's sake!'

Molly bounded away, unnerved by his rage.

'Bil, you're scaring me. What's happening?'

'What's happening is that fucking junkie couldn't do *one* thing right!'

Dread squeezed her chest. 'What did you do?' She watched his face tense with rage. 'Bil, what did you do?'

'I asked him to do one fucking thing!'

'What did you do?' Her voice was a whisper.

'It wasn't meant to happen like this. He was just meant to mess things up.'

'Rich?' Salma struggled to fit the pieces. 'How?'

'I paid him to get Molly back.'

Salma blinked. 'But you said they left her there.'

'I paid them to leave. I didn't want you to know that. It's just so fucking *pathetic*.' Bil's face was full of disgust. 'Then the police raided our house and I was so *angry* at Tom and Willa. Were we just meant to accept what they did to our son?' Bil gritted his teeth. 'I gave Rich money to trash Tom's house. I told him to use the loose plank in our fence to get into their garden. How could I have known that Zain would be in their house? He's usually on Twitch at that time.'

Salma stared at him. 'You,' she said breathlessly. 'You did this?'

'Rich got spooked when he found Zain in Jamie's bedroom. He tried to get away but Zain chased him onto the balcony. There was a struggle and that's when Zain fell.'

114

Salma's mind was blank with shock.

'Rich was about to flee when Tom came home. He ran back upstairs and hopped across onto Zain's balcony.'

'Zain's balcony?' she asked dumbly.

Bil choked on his next words. 'He was still here when we got home. I hid him in Zain's bathroom. I panicked, Salma. I didn't know what to do.'

'You knew,' she said with a note of wonder. 'You watched me cry and pray and *beg* to understand, and you *knew* all this time.' She bent forward, gripped by a crippling rage.

'*They* did this, Salma. Not me.'

'They didn't do this!' she roared. 'They didn't nearly kill my son!'

'These people. They want to break us and they push and they push and they push. Well, I broke, Salma. They broke me.'

His despair added to Salma's own. Her husband was a man who followed the rules but had been driven to an act of ... what? Revenge? Rebellion? Madness?

'Salma, *please*. It was an accident.'

'You let me think that Tom hurt our son.' Guilt fired inside her. Tom had been wrongly convicted. 'You have to tell the police.'

Bil stared at her. 'No.' There was no argument in his tone. Just plain, simple refusal. He knelt by the fridge and reached for the phone, grunting with effort. 'I searched for this thing everywhere. Rich said he dropped it and I searched and searched for it.' Bil plucked up a large knife and swept it back and forth beneath the fridge. There was a dull thunk and, slowly, carefully, he pulled out the phone.

'Bil, you have to tell the police.'

'We can't do that,' he said calmly. 'We've come too far. I paid Rich, I lied in court, I …' He fell quiet.

Salma sensed something awful. 'Oh God, Bil, what did you do?' She looked at the phone and was hit by a sick possibility. 'Rich?'

Bil didn't answer. He knelt by the sink and took out a hammer from the cupboard below. He wrapped the phone in a tea towel and raised the hammer above it.

'Bil, did you hurt that boy?' Salma asked urgently. The hammer trembled in his hand. 'Bil, you didn't … Did you kill that boy?'

A bead of sweat dripped off his forehead. 'No,' he said. 'But I was there.'

'Why?' whispered Salma.

'He was blackmailing me. He said he would tell the police. I knew he wouldn't admit to a crime, but then he started using *you*. He said he would tell you and started demanding money. I went to see him one day to give him some cash and he had clearly taken something. His skin looked clammy and he fell asleep. I took out my phone to call the police, but how could I explain what I was doing there?'

'And?'

'And I left him there.'

Salma felt a fresh wave of horror. 'Did you know that he was dying?'

It took Bil a moment to answer. 'I suspected.'

Salma felt a rush of nausea. 'I have no idea who you are.'

Bil took a step towards her. He must have seen her flinch because he quickly put down the hammer. 'Salma, it's me.'

'You're not going to get away with this. They'll catch you.'

'Not if we keep quiet.'

She shook her head wildly. 'You can't let Tom rot in jail.'

'Why not?'

'Because—' Salma froze when she heard a creak by the garden door. They both looked up to see Jamie in the kitchen. The air turned electric. Bil reached for the hammer and Salma spoke urgently. 'Bil, he can't hear.'

Bil studied Jamie who looked like a deer in head-lights. He gripped the handle of the hammer. 'He can hear well enough.'

Salma shook her head at Jamie to tell him to stay calm. For a moment, it seemed he would listen, but a primal instinct got the best of him and he turned on his heel and fled.

'Jamie, no!'

Bil threw the hammer and it caught Jamie's shoulder blade. He stumbled and crashed into the kitchen table with an ugly crack. Bil was on Jamie in a second. He pinned a knee against his torso and covered his nose and mouth. Salma shrieked in panic. She bolted over and clawed at Bil's arm.

'You're going to kill him!' She threw all her weight against him. 'Bil, stop it!'

He groped for the hammer and Salma watched in horror as he raised it above his head. 'No!' she screamed and crashed forward, forcing the blow off course. The fat steel head of the hammer skimmed her temple and she felt it explode in pain. As she dropped to the floor, she sensed that Jamie wasn't moving. In a daze, she thought she saw an angel in white glide into the room. It lifted something above Bil's head. But then the image faded and her body gave in to the pain.

Chapter Thirty

Salma's mouth was dry and the air felt too warm. There was a scent in the air: baby formula or something sweet and milky. She opened her eyes and blinked away the sleep. She tried to sit up, but grew still when she saw who was in the chair opposite.

'You're awake,' said Willa.

Salma sat up too quickly and winced from the pain. 'Where's my son?' she asked croakily.

'He's okay. He's here in the hospital.'

A cold feeling came over Salma. 'Bil?'

'He confessed. The police have arrested him.'

Salma closed her eyes. The room seemed to sway around her, making her feel seasick.

'It's okay,' said Willa.

On hearing this tiny kindness, Salma began to cry. Her sobs were low and hopeless, like a trapped animal's.

'I saw you, Salma. I saw you save Jamie.' Willa's voice was thick with sorrow. 'I've been such a witch to you. Why would you help me?'

'What could I do?' said Salma. 'Let this war go on? Where would it stop?'

Willa smoothed her white dress. 'I wish we could have been friends, Salma. I really think we would have been if you hadn't assumed the worst of Tom and we hadn't—'

Salma looked up sharply. 'Tom is not innocent, Willa. He targeted my family again and again.'

Willa exhaled slowly as if building her nerve. 'I need to tell you something.' She fiddled with her diamond ring. 'Tom didn't send the squatters to your restaurant. I did. Rich was dropping off some weed and I mentioned that your place was empty.'

'You?' Salma blinked. 'Why would you do that?'

'And I was the one who took your dog,' said Willa, keen now to confess. 'She kept coming into our garden and it was a spur-of-the-moment thing. I was angry that you had got Tom fired, so I gave Molly to Rich. It was only meant to be for a day.'

Salma stared at her, unable to make sense of her cruelty.

'And it was me who reported the knives,' she said. 'I'm sorry. I didn't think it through.'

The words hit Salma like a wrecking ball. 'You need to leave,' she told Willa.

'You're not listening. I'm trying to say I'm sorry.'

'You need to leave.' Salma pressed the call button.

'Jesus, you *like* being angry, don't you? You're not the only person who lost something, Salma. *I* lost my baby.'

'Get out.' Salma's voice was low and dangerous. 'Get. Out.' When Willa didn't move, Salma lost her temper. 'Get out!' She swiped at a jug of water, which flew across the room and bounced off the wall in a clatter.

Willa sprang to her feet. She ran into the corridor and found a nurse. 'Can we have some help please? My friend is having a panic attack.'

On hearing this, Salma began to shout. She pulled away from the nurse and knocked over a vase. It smashed onto the floor and glass flew everywhere.

'Just calm down,' said the nurse. Salma shoved her hand away.

'Please give her something,' said Willa.

'No!' shouted Salma, but the nurse was already pushing a needle into her arm. Salma's head hit the pillow and she sank back to sleep.

Chapter Thirty-One

Jamie watched Zain's heartbeat on the hospital monitor. All these months he had blamed himself for leaving Zain alone that day. Jamie had secretly worried that his dad was, in fact, guilty. He could picture it. His dad finding Zain in the house, Zain getting mouthy, his dad grabbing Zain, and Zain fighting back.

Jamie had watched his father a hundred times looking for signs of guilt. He had never seen one and now he knew why. Because Bil was the one who was guilty. Bil had paid Rich to trash the house. And Rich was the one who pushed Zain.

Jamie watched him now as he lay in the hospital bed. 'I wish I could change things,' he said. He reached out to touch Zain's hand but hovered just above it. 'I wish I had just punched you that day. You would have gone home and none of this would have happened. Instead I did what I always do.' Jamie thought back to that day.

Zain had enjoyed insulting him. He had pushed Jamie's chest and laughed when he raised his fists because it was so clear that he had no idea what to do with them. Jamie had stood there, hot with shame, trying to hold back tears. He had really thought that Zain would hit him, but then he realised that Zain was fighting back tears as well. Jamie had felt relief but Zain had only got angrier. He had smacked the wall and stormed off.

'Wait,' Jamie had stopped him. He knew that if Zain left, their friendship would never recover. 'I talked to Camilla,' he had said quickly. 'It was only for a minute but *she* came up to *me*.'

Zain's confusion had lifted him out of his mood. 'Camilla?' he'd said. 'The girl you like?'

Jamie had smiled crookedly. 'Yeah.' He had talked and talked until he saw Zain relax. That's when the alarm had interrupted them. 'Shit, I've got to get to tutoring.' Jamie had looked at Zain with a question. 'We've still got to upload the demo.'

'I'll get it done.'

'Use my computer. It'll be quicker.'

Zain had made a face. 'What about your parents?'

'They're out.'

'And what if they come home and find me here?' Zain had sliced a finger across his throat.

Jamie had laughed. 'Don't worry. I'll be back in an hour.'

And with that, Zain's fate was sealed.

Chapter Thirty-Two

Salma sat across from Bil in the chilly prison hall. She couldn't believe how much he had aged in the last four months alone. His hair was greying and his skin seemed loose around the jowls. She reached across the table and took his hand. She hadn't forgiven him, but she still loved him. The man she had married was *real*, and worthy of the life she had shared with him. He had to pay for what he did, but she didn't want prison to break him. Three long years at Pentonville for perverting the course of justice.

'Will you ever forgive me?' he asked her.

Salma tried to be kind. 'I need Zain to wake up,' she said. 'Until that happens …' she shook her head.

'I can't do this alone, Salma.'

Salma pulled her hand back. 'I need more time.'

'Do you still love me?'

'That's not fair, Bil.'

'Do you?'

'Of course I do. I can't just switch it off.'

'Then wait for me, Salma. Please.'

She closed her eyes and hot tears rolled down her cheek. 'I don't know how to rebuild.'

'Together,' he said in an urgent whisper. 'We rebuild together.'

The sound of a klaxon rang through the room. Visiting hours were over. Bil stood and pulled her into a hug. She let him hold her, but her body remained stiff. She said goodbye and left without kissing him. That was a kindness she couldn't yet give.

At home, the first thing she did was shower, scrubbing off the smell of prison in case Zain could sense it. She checked on him, switched on his baby monitor and gave him a kiss on the cheek. 'We'll be back in thirty,' she told him. She pulled on a heavy coat and clipped on Molly's leash. Outside, the air was cool with the first signs of autumn.

She spotted a moving van parked outside the house next door. A man and a woman were halfway across the lawn, heaving a grey sofa. She locked eyes with the man.

'Hi!' he called. He was in his early forties with a square jaw and muscular shoulders. He said something to the woman and they set down the sofa. They walked over and introduced themselves as Matthew and Jenny Law.

'This is such a lovely street,' said Jenny.

'Yes, it is,' said Salma. 'You'll be very happy here.'

Jenny looked up at Matthew. 'I hope so,' she said with shining eyes. 'I'm so pleased we met you. Everyone else seems retired and we were starting to worry!'

Salma laughed politely.

'It's a shame that Tom and Willa moved out. They seemed like such a nice couple.'

Salma nodded. 'A shame.'

'Did you know them well?'

'Well enough.'

Jenny took Matthew's hand and lifted it sportingly. 'Well, I hope we can fill their boots.'

'I'm sure,' said Salma. Next to her, Molly barked, making the three of them laugh.

'Well, it was lovely to meet you,' said Jenny.

'You too. Welcome to Hampton.' She said goodbye and headed up the street with Molly. She enjoyed the crunch of leaves underfoot. More than spring, this was a time of renewal: some things dying and clearing away, making space for new. The air was crisp and Salma felt a weight lift off her. For the first time that year, she felt hopeful about the future.

Molly tugged at her leash and Salma eased her along. A few steps further, she stopped and sighed. 'Molly, I forgot your bags.' She turned and jogged back home, shushing Molly's whine. She let herself into the house and grabbed two, then three, plastic bags and tucked them into her pocket. When she stepped out again, something caught her eye: a small red-and-white flag stuck in her new neighbours' plant pot. She tensed at the sight of the St George's Cross. She watched it for a moment, fluttering in the breeze. She went up to it and lightly touched the fabric. Then, she tugged it out of the soil. The tiny flagpole was surprisingly heavy. She traced a fingertip along the seams. Then, she folded it neatly and tossed it onto their lawn. She and Molly headed to the park without looking back.

Acknowledgements

I wrote *Those People Next Door* in the deep pandemic and could not have done it without Peter Watson who listened to me fret and whine on our long and rambling walks. Thank you for never letting me feel sorry for myself.

Jessica Faust, you are the sort of woman that I aspire to be: tough and efficient but somehow also kind and patient. Thank you for everything.

Thank you to Manpreet Grewal without whom I would not have a career. You're a street fighter and I'm so bloody grateful to have you in my corner.

Thank you to Lisa Milton for your guts and determination but also your warmth. I wish you could hear all the wonderful things that people say about you when you're not in the room.

Thank you to The Reading Agency and everyone involved in the Quick Reads scheme. Reading changed my life and I am honoured to be a part of this year's programme.

Thank you to everyone at HQ. I'm so lucky

to work with people who feel more like friends than colleagues.

A special thank you to Peter Borcsok and the team at HarperCollins Canada who always come out to bat for me.

Thank you to Mary Alice Kier, James McGowan and the BookEnds team. Thank you, also, to Eldes Tran for sorting my tidbits from my titbits and generally making me look good.

I am indebted to so many who helped me with their time and expertise. Thank you, Graham Bartlett, Dina Begum, Matthew Butt QC, Kelly Corp, Sairish Hussain, Hiren Joshi, Nadine Matheson, Dr Daniel Wilbor, Dr Claire Windeatt and Dr Michael Yoong. As ever, I hope you will forgive me for any errors I've made or creative license I've taken with your meticulous advice.

Thank you to all my fellow authors that have championed my work. There are so many of you that have done so much. I dare not try and name you all but I hope you know that I'm so incredibly grateful that you have taken the time to read and share my work.

A special thank you to all the booksellers, librarians, reviewers and bloggers that have shared my books with readers. Historically, there's been debate about whether names like mine on a cover can sell. Every time you have sold, loaned, shared or recommended my book, you have made a difference and for that I am deeply grateful.

Thank you, as ever, to my sisters Reena, Jay, Shopna, Forida and Shafia.

Finally, thank you to you, the reader, for picking up this copy of *Those People Next Door*. I hope you'll find me online to share what you're reading next.

THE READING AGENCY | **Quick Reads**

About Quick Reads

"Reading is such an important building block for success"
~ Jojo Moyes

Quick Reads are short books written
by best-selling authors.

Did you enjoy this Quick Read?

Tell us what you thought by filling in
our short survey. Scan the **QR code**
to go directly to the survey or
visit **bit.ly/QR2024**

Thanks to Penguin Random House and Hachette and to all
our publishing partners for their ongoing support.

A special thankyou to Jojo Moyes for her generous donation in
2020-2022 which helped to build the future of Quick Reads.

Quick Reads is delivered by The Reading Agency, a UK charity
with a mission to get people fired up about reading, because
everything changes when you read.

www.readingagency.org.uk   @readingagency   #QuickReads

The Reading Agency Ltd. Registered number: 3904882 (England & Wales)
Registered charity number: 1085443 (England & Wales)
Registered Office: 24 Bedford Row, London, WC1R 4EH
The Reading Agency is supported using public funding by
Arts Council England.

Supported using public funding by
**ARTS COUNCIL
ENGLAND**

THE READING AGENCY | Quick Reads

Find your next Quick Read...

For 2024 we have selected 6 popular
Quick Reads for you to enjoy!

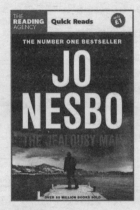

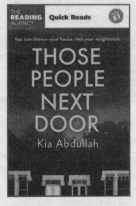

Quick Reads are available to buy in paperback or ebook and to borrow from your local library. For a complete list of titles and more information on the authors and their books visit **www.readingagency.org.uk/quickreads**

Continue your reading journey with The Reading Agency:

Reading Ahead

Challenge yourself to complete six reads by taking part in **Reading Ahead** at your local library, college or workplace: **readingahead.org.uk**

Reading
Groups
for Everyone

Join **Reading Groups for Everyone** to find a reading group and discover new books: **readinggroups.org.uk**

World Book Night

Celebrate reading on **World Book Night** every year on 23 April: **worldbooknight.org**

Summer Reading Challenge

Read with your family as part of the **Summer Reading Challenge: summerreadingchallenge.org.uk**

For more information on our work and the power of reading please visit our website: **readingagency.org.uk**

More from Quick Reads

If you enjoyed the 2024 Quick Reads please explore our 6 titles from 2023.

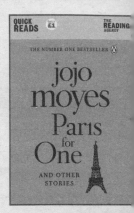

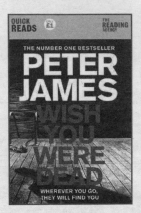

For a complete list of titles and more information on the authors and their books visit:

www.readingagency.org.uk/quickreads

Kia Abdullah is a bestselling author and travel writer. Her novels include *Take It Back*, a *Guardian* and *Telegraph* thriller of the year; *Truth Be Told*, and *Next of Kin*. Kia has also been selected for *The Times* Crime Club.

For more information about Kia and her writing, visit her website at kiaabdullah.com, or follow her at @KiaAbdullah on Instagram and X.

This novel is entirely a work of fiction. The names, characters and incidents portrayed in it are the work of the author's imagination. Any resemblance to actual persons, living or dead, events or localities is entirely coincidental.

HQ
An imprint of HarperCollins*Publishers* Ltd
1 London Bridge Street
London SE1 9GF

www.harpercollins.co.uk

HarperCollins*Publishers*
Macken House, 39/40 Mayor Street Upper,
Dublin 1, D01 C9W8, Ireland

This Quick Reads edition 2024

1
First published in Great Britain by
HQ, an imprint of HarperCollins*Publishers* Ltd 2024

Copyright © Kia Abdullah 2024

Kia Abdullah asserts the moral right to be
identified as the author of this work.
A catalogue record for this book is
available from the British Library.

ISBN: 978-0-00-865434-4

This book contains FSC™ certified paper and other controlled
sources to ensure responsible forest management.

For more information visit: www.harpercollins.co.uk/green

This book is set in 12/16 pt. Stone Serif by Type-it AS, Norway

Printed and Bound in the UK using 100% Renewable Electricity at
CPI Group (UK) Ltd, Croydon, CR0 4YY